The Chronicles of Stella Rice:

CARNAL HEAT

By

Adrienne Kama

Contemporary Romantic Erotica

New Concepts   Georgia

Be sure to check out our website for the very best in fiction at fantastic prices!

When you visit our webpage, you can:
* Read excerpts of currently available books
* View cover art of upcoming books and current releases
* Find out more about the talented artists who capture the magic of the writer's imagination on the covers
* Order books from our backlist
* Find out the latest NCP and author news--including any upcoming book signings by your favorite NCP author
* Read author bios and reviews of our books
* Get NCP submission guidelines
* And so much more!

We offer a 20% discount on all new Trade Paperback releases ordered from our website!

Be sure to visit our webpage to find the best deals in e-books and paperbacks! To find out about our new releases as soon as they are available, please be sure to sign up for our newsletter (http://www.newconceptspublishing.com/newsletter.htm) or join our reader group (http://groups.yahoo.com/group/new_concepts_pub/join)!

The newsletter is available by double opt in only and our customer information is *never* shared!

Visit our webpage at:
www.newconceptspublishing.com

Carnal Heat is a publication of NCP. This work is a novel. Any similarity to actual persons or events is purely coincidental.

New Concepts Publishing, Inc.
5202 Humphreys Rd.
Lake Park, GA 31636

ISBN 1-58608-885-8
© 2006 Adrienne Kama
Cover art (c) copyright 2006 Eliza Black

NCP books are available at special quantity discounts for bulk purchases for sales promotions, premiums, fund raising, or educational use. For details, write, email, or phone New Concepts Publishing, Inc., 5202 Humphreys Rd., Lake Park, GA 31636; Ph. 229-257-0367, Fax 229-219-1097; orders@newconceptspublishing.com.

First NCP Trade Paperback Printing: November 2006

Dedication:

For Amy, Kat, and Melsy, who throughout the years have showed me the meaning of friendship. You mean more to me than you'll ever know.

Authors note:

The Chronicles of Stella Rice is a work of fiction. While casual sex is not lethal in Stella's world, it is deadly in our own. Please practice safe sex.

Chapter One

Journal Entry 3/5/05; 7:19 AM

My name is Stella Rice. I'm thirty, I live in Baltimore, and I co-own and run a successful business support services company with my friend Ann. AIR--Accurate Individualized Resources--is one of the most important things in my life. Between creating multi-media presentations for large corporations and writing eye-catching resumes for job seekers, I stay pretty busy. Add to that regular dinner dates with my three best girlfriends, Ann, Katarina, and Meagan and anyone can see I have a very happy, very fulfilling life. Anyone, that is, except maybe my mother, my sisters, and my extended family. It's knowing what my family would think of me if they knew what I'd been up to that makes me to wonder what in the hell I'm doing.

Okay, so I know what I'm doing. I'm dating two men. But why am I dating two men? Because they're fun, sexy, handsome, fantastic in bed, funny, intelligent, I could go on. I could list dozens of reasons why Jake and Dev are important to me. What I can't do is come up with a reason good enough to tell my mother.

I'm dating two men!

How long can I hide this from my family?

* * * *

7:31 AM

So I'm dating two men. Big deal. I'm sure I'm not the first, and I won't be the last. Hey, men do this kind of thing all the time--dating two women at the same time. Sure, usually one woman doesn't know about the other, but that's beside the point. It's 2005 for crying out loud! There's nothing wrong with what I'm doing. I must be doing something right if I've managed to attract not one, but two incredible men. Right now I'm feeling pretty damn good about myself and I'm determined to enjoy it. Who knows how long this'll last?

I am woman, hear me roar!

I'd met Jake back in January when I'd joined his gym, Fit For Life, as a way to meet men with Katarina. Unfortunately, Katarina and I made the mistake of taking Jake's kickboxing class. He'd been the kickboxing instructor from hell and each class was so exhausting that we were always too tired to do anything afterwards except escape. Then, something unexpected had happened. Jake, fitness guru of Baltimore, seduced me. Or should I say SEDUCED, all caps, because what he did to me had truly blown my mind. And that's not all. Big, tough, strong Jake wasn't just a sexual genius, he was also bisexual and in love with a man. Initially I'd been crushed to find out Jake was in a long-term relationship with someone else. I hadn't felt so connected to a guy since I'd been with my high school sweetheart, Steven Howard, and that was saying a lot. Finding out Jake not only lived an alternative lifestyle but lived it with someone he loved was a blow. Then another, far stranger thing occurred. I'd met Jake's boyfriend, Dev and … well, they both sort of seduced me. And I'd sort of been seeing them both ever since.

My sex life has never been better!

Oh crap, the phone.

I hope it's not my mother. Haven't told her about the new turn my life has taken … and I don't plan to. I'm not telling her or any of my sisters. They'd kill me.

Argh! There it is again.

Maybe it's one of the girls.

Let's hope.

* * * *

8:23 AM

Argh! Why did I pick it up! It was her, my mother. Crap! And I know she knows something's up. She was asking questions. How's my personal life? Do I have plans for the weekend? Stuff like that. I'm convinced my mother wasted the best years of her life not studying law. She knows good and well she could have had a lucrative career at the NSA. Nobody can scope out information better than my mother … well, maybe Oprah Winfrey.

I dodged as best as I could but I think she's on to me. I *cannot* let her find out I'm dating two men. That would be a disaster. I have enough to think about as it is, i.e., how to keep two very large, very healthy, very sexual men happy.

Gotta go for now. The shower and coffee are calling … and my mom said she'll be here at noon.

* * * *

3:22 PM

"Stella! Are you still single, girl? You better hurry up and find someone. You know you're not getting any younger."

I raised my flute of Riesling and tried to focus on the crisp, fragrant liquid sloshing around the glass. I hadn't been home for two hours and already I'd been asked if I'd found a man, was pregnant yet, and had been informed that I was gaining weight.

Have I said how much I hate going home?

I'd grown up in Laurel, Maryland, in a big old Victorian on Montgomery Street a few blocks over from Main. Despite how much I loathed going home, the house itself was nice. Quaint even. There was a pretty side porch where I used to spend summers as a little girl, playing with dolls and staring up at the violets my mother hung from the picket rails. The house had three, tri-level gables, a three-story turret that could have been taken straight out of a fairy-tale, and a lushly landscaped front lawn that in the summer was bright with yellow roses and pink orchids. For as long as I'd been alive it had been home to me, my four older sisters (Alyssa, Jackie, Reese, and Robin), and my mom. I'd had some of my best experiences in this house. My first kiss with Steven Howard, first time I'd had sex had been in my attic bedroom … again with Steven Howard, my first sleepover had been in this house with Katarina and Meagan who'd both grown up a few houses down from me. A lot of great things had happened in this house. Unfortunately, because it was so large, it was also the congregation spot of choice for my extended family. That meant seeing my annoying cousin Sadie on a regular basis.

"Shut up, Sadie," my sister Alyssa said, nudging Sadie with a pointy elbow. She set the bowl of cooked potatoes she was holding on the dining room table, and then slid into the seat beside me to mash them. "My baby sister doesn't need a man. She owns her own business, owns her home, and is perfectly fine being by herself. Isn't that right, baby girl?"

(Yep! You read that right. She called me baby girl. It's one of the indignities I'll have to suffer through for the rest of my life. I'll be ninety-nine and my older sisters will still be calling me 'baby girl.')

Sadie rolled her eyes and fingered her shoulder length, brown hair. "I'm sure. All I know is that by the time I was her age," she jabbed a finger in my direction, "I was married with my fourth baby on the way. Maybe if you fixed yourself up a bit, Stella. You know you can't go out wearing a bun. Men won't be paying you any attention if you look like that. And those jeans look about two sizes too big for you."

Have I said how much I hate my cousin Sadie? The cow! Having mistaken my mother's house for a nightclub, she'd come wearing a micro-mini, Chaka Khan hair, a frilly red blouse, and fuck-me pumps.

"I like my bun," I offered, wondering who she'd bribed to watch the aforementioned spawn. She'd shown up at my mother's door without them or her husband. Come to think of it; lately, I hadn't seen that much of Stanley. Maybe he'd finally had enough of Sadie and her whiny offspring and hit the road. Couldn't say I'd have blamed him.

"Don't take offense, Stella. I'm just saying. You know you better hurry up and find yourself a man. You know I'm right."

"Maybe I don't want a man."

Dressed in her signature Chic jeans, my mother stumbled into the room, hand fixed melodramatically to her breast. Her short, raven hair bobbed as she cantered to the left, lost her footing, and nearly smacked her head against the glass doors of the china cabinet.

Alyssa was on her feet and at my mother's side in two strides. Reluctantly, I followed. "Are you all right, mommy?"

She slapped the steadying hand I'd placed on her shoulder as though I were a troublesome gnat. "Don't you ever say that, Stella," she roared, peering heavenward as though God would curse me to eternal spinsterhood for daring to say such a thing. "Of course you want a man. You just haven't found the right one yet."

I rolled my eyes.

"Don't you roll your eyes at me, Stella Marie Rice. How long has it been since you've been to church anyway? You never rolled your eyes when you lived at home and went to church. You were a good girl when you lived at home and went to church."

Argh! It was like being sixteen all over again. "I didn't roll my eyes," I explained, lying through my teeth. "I must have gotten an eyelash in my eye or something."

"You can't give up," Sadie continued, doggedly. "There's a man out there for you."

Ha! That's where she was wrong. Turns out there were two men out there for me. For about a millisecond I considered telling them as much, but quickly decided doing so wouldn't be in my best interest. In her present state, my mom was likely to faint dead away. Instead, I asked Sadie, "So where's Stan?"

The cow's face went blank. You'd think she'd never heard the name before.

"You know, Stan. About this tall," I raised a hand over my head, "and married to you. The father of your children ... am I ringing any bells?"

Her upper lip curled. "You think I don't know my own husband? He took the girls to the aquarium."

"Likely excuse."

My mother eyed me. "Stella, Stella." She shook her head sadly and sighed. "Stop annoying your cousin. Go to the kitchen and help your sisters."

Thusly chastised, I walked into the kitchen, side-stepped my sisters, snuck out the far side, and went in search of my purse.

Five minutes later I was locked in the upstairs bathroom with my cell phone, staring out the window over the bathtub at the steadily falling snow, and trying desperately to speak quiet enough so I wouldn't be overheard.

"We'll see you tomorrow night," Jake was saying. "Just think about that."

"I know," I whispered, "but I want to see you now. I can't take it anymore. My family is going to make me crazy."

"You've only been there a couple of hours. It can't be that bad."

I'd hoped calling Jake would help me to feel better, but hearing that deep, sultry voice was making me even more desperate to get away from my family. "They keep telling me I should meet a man."

"Well tell them you have. Tell them you've met two."

Just the thought of what my mother would do were she to find out about Jake and Dev made me break out in a cold sweat. "Are you crazy! She'd kill me."

Jake laughed. "Are we really that bad?"

"Of course not. It's not me, it's her. She wouldn't understand. She's Catholic," I said that last bit as though it would explain everything.

Apparently it did. "Oh. Well, you do realize you'll have to tell her sometime, that is if you intend for this relationship to go anywhere. You can't hide us forever."

Forever, hell. It had only been a few weeks. Give a girl some time to adjust to being in a ménage for crying out loud. "I don't intend to. It's just … shit! Someone's coming. I gotta go." I flipped my phone shut and was on my feet so fast I got light headed.

"Stella! Baby girl, are you in there?"

My sister, Jackie. "Yeah. Is dinner done already?"

A few seconds ticked by before she answered. "Yeah. And you've got a visitor."

A visitor?

* * * *

5:01 PM

"So how have you been, Stella? Your mom tells me you live in Baltimore now." Steven Howard spooned mashed potatoes and gravy and popped them into his mouth.

I couldn't believe it. I simply could not believe it. What had she been thinking? If she'd deliberately set out to humiliate me she couldn't have done a better job. I wanted the floor to open up and suck me in. My mother had invited my high school boyfriend to dinner. Did she have any idea how pathetic that made me look? And she'd done it without uttering so much as a word to me. It was unforgivable.

Mouth full of baked ham, I nodded. Silently, I throttled myself for wearing my hair in a bun. Had I known he'd be over for dinner I would have worn it down. And I wouldn't have worn my frayed CK jeans or the oversized sweater. I looked exactly like the spinster my mother lived in fear that I'd become.

"And you own your own business." Dressed in crisp black slacks, a navy shirt, with his micro braids flowing sexily to the middle of his back, Steven smiled at me from across the table. His smooth brown skin was flawless. I didn't think he had aged a year since I'd last seen him.

Waggling her eyebrows like the desperate cow she was, cousin Sadie edged her chair closer to Steven. Another inch and she'd be sitting in his lap. "I'm surprised some lucky lady hasn't snatched you up, Stevie." Sadie announced to the table at large. "You were always the most handsome boy at school."

"I was married … briefly," he said. "But things didn't work out."

"Stella's never been married."

Alyssa's hand clamped around my forearm, pulling me back into my seat. I considered dumping my fruit punch on Sadie, but decided against it. My mother would never forgive me.

Steven arched a brow. "I find that hard to believe, Stella."

Sadie snorted. "Believe it."

"You're just as pretty as you were in high school, Stella."

Seeing things running as she'd planned, my mother beamed. "Stella was always a pretty girl. Well, she was after she got through that awkward stage. She was the most beautiful baby in the hospital."

"Huh!" Sadie muttered. "Anyone looks good with a weave."

My mouth fell open. For a second I wished I was sixteen again. If I were sixteen it would have been more acceptable for me to leap across the table and shove a plate full of mashed potatoes in Sadie's face. When you're thirty, however, behavior like that isn't tolerated. So I gritted my teeth and strove for calm. "I don't wear a weave."

Over in the far end of the living room, at the kids table, a series of giggles rose from my nieces and nephews.

"Next thing, you'll be telling us your bra isn't padded either."

I shoved away from the table and rocketed to my feet, my face hot with indignation.

Alyssa yanked me back into my seat. "So Steven, what have you been up to since we last saw you?"

I could feel my mother's eyes boring into me so I made a point not to look in her direction.

Sadie smirked, and then edged closer to Steven.

Long accustomed to my family, Steven rolled on as though nothing had happened.

I was too annoyed to follow the conversation after that. I longed to kick Sadie, was dizzy with my need to throttle her. I was so wrapped up in imagining various ways I could maim and torture her that I didn't notice the sway of the conversation until it was too late.

"You know Stella's birthday is coming," my mother was saying. "We're throwing an intimate dinner party for her here at the house. If you're not busy we'd love it if you'd come."

I looked up in time to see Steven nod. "I'd love to. I'm honored to be invited."

"Don't you think I'm getting too old for birthday parties, mommy?" I queried.

My mother waved this off. "Don't be ridiculous, Stella. You're my little girl and I want to have a birthday dinner for my little girl," she beamed at Steven. "Then it's settled. You're coming to Stella's birthday dinner. Do you remember what day her birthday is?"

Right on cue, Steven said, "April fifteenth."

Argh!

* * * *

11:22 PM

In bed now and not sure what I should tell Jake and Dev about this whole birthday thing. One thing I know for sure, I can't bring them to my mother's house. She'd have a fit. I mean, literally, have a fit. Problem is, I don't think Jake or Dev would be thrilled to find out I'm spending my birthday with my ex-boyfriend, especially an ex-boyfriend as good looking as Steven.

Steven and I had met back in high school. I was a sixteen year old, recovering geek and he'd been a seventeen year old, musical prodigy with good looks, charm, and a restored 69' Mustang. We'd met on the school concourse in front of the auditorium during a particularly painful production of A Christmas Carol. I'd left my class to run to the bathroom and Steven had sort of boycotted the whole thing because the lead roll of Ebenezer Scrooge had gone to the less talented Timmy Colin. He'd been stationed on a bench in the grassy knoll at the center of the concourse, glaring at the auditorium doors when I'd come out. When he saw me he'd angled a jean clad leg and sneaker on the bench and he sat up. "How's it going in there?"

I can't say whether it was my new contact lenses, the rose colored lip-gloss I was wearing, or my cool new hairstyle, but I walked over to the bench, mini-skirt swooshing, smiled, and told the hottest guy in school that, "It would be much better if you were in it. Timmy sucks as Scrooge."

"I knew it. I tried to tell Mrs. Cooter but she wouldn't listen."

I'd nodded sagely. "Bet she wishes she had."

Steven had scooted over on the bench and smiled up at me. "Wanna sit?"

I did. And from that point on, we'd been inseparable. Least we had been until Steven had decided to run off to Berklee College of Music in Boston after graduation. Berklee had pretty much been the end of us.

Pushing thoughts of Steven and the entire day aside, I rolled over in bed and closed my eyes. "Think I'll sleep on it."

Chapter Two

Journal Entry 3/8/05; 7:41 PM

"Okay, so who is your favorite Brad?" Meagan pushed her long, honey blonde curls off her shoulders, stepped back, and gave me a once over. Her full lips were drawn down in a frown over her smooth coffee and cream complexion, and she had one hand on her voluptuous, rayon sheathed hip. I knew instantly she didn't like what I had on. "Still think the dress is too long, Stella. You should put something else on."

We were in my bedroom and had been for the last two hours. Ann, Katarina, and Meagan had come over to help me get ready for my first official date with Jake and Dev. Though I'd been seeing the two of them for a while, I was oddly nervous about this whole date thing, and my friends knew it. Katarina, despite her flowing blonde-bombshell hair, was decidedly prudish about the entire situation. She thought the Jake/Dev situation was "too icky." But she'd come over anyway, determined to support me even though she was convinced I was making a mistake. This was a position Meagan pretty much agreed with. On the other end of the spectrum was Ann. Ann, chestnut locks curling over the collar of her forest green turtleneck, was of the opinion that it was about time one of us did something daring. As the only one in the group who'd been in a relationship for the last two years I wasn't surprised. Ann was engaged now, and though she and her boyfriend Gerard had endured a rough time last month, Ann was always looking for some type of excitement, even if it was through me.

Ann had closed the blinds and turned on every light in my bedroom, this way I could be scrutinized from every conceivable angle. Katarina was busy choosing shades of lipstick from my vanity. She was making a lot of noise throwing aside colors she thought were dated. "Definitely the *Legends-of-the-Fall* Brad Pitt. He was hot in that one."

Meagan gripped the seam of my dress and hiked it up until I felt warm air on my backside. "I'd have to go with *Interview with the Vampire,* Brad," she said as she surveyed the results. "Brad looks good with long hair, doesn't he?"

"No, Meagan." I stared in horror at my bared thighs, and then stepped away from her. At its normal length, my dress fell just below my thighs. It had spaghetti straps and was backless. With its sheer, lushly red material and swooping neckline, it was one of the sexiest things I owned. No way was it too long. If I wore the dress the way Meagan wanted and bent over tonight, I was likely to give everyone around me a peep show.

Suddenly uninterested in the proceedings, Ann stretched out on my bed, laid her head against my collection of pillows so her hair fanned out around her, then yawned. With a languid shuffling of her jean clad legs, she folded them at the ankle and stared up at the ceiling. "You're both wrong. The hottest Brad was definitely *Fight Club,* Brad. Gerard hates *Fight Club.* He says the ending was stupid and I tell him that's beside the point. Brad Pitt sweaty, shirtless, and rolling all over the floor with other sweaty and shirtless men is the point."

Ann's boyfriend Gerard had been such a fixture in Ann's life that he was practically one of the girls now. He often went out for drinks with us and to the movies. I'd actually expected to see him tonight, but he'd had to work late.

Gerard was a very cool boyfriend. The polar opposite of Katarina's boyfriend, Jim.

Jim, who wasn't working late but hadn't been invited, was a relatively new addition to our lives. Katarina had met Jim at Jake's gym the same time I'd met Jake. Unlike Gerard, who was laid-back and easy going, Jim was nearly as clingy as Katarina. Together, the two were bearable only in small doses. When together they moved about as though joined at the hip. It was like they were conjoined twins or something.

"Come sit, Stella. I found one." Katarina motioned me to the vanity and pointed at the overstuffed chair. She was careful to make sure I sat facing away from the mirror. No doubt so I couldn't see what she was doing to me. "Jim hates anything with Brad Pitt in it. The only Brad movie he's ever watched with me was *Twelve Monkeys,* and that movie just doesn't count." She pulled out a few of my drawers then frowned at me. "Where do you keep your mascara? It wasn't with the rest of your make-up."

When I told her, "I don't wear mascara," I thought she'd keel over and die of shock.

"Don't wear mascara! Why not?"

I shrugged. "I don't know. It's too much trouble."

"Brad looked a little too rough in that movie for me," Meagan said, completely ignoring Katarina and me.

Ann nodded. "Yeah, but his chest never looked better. The things I could do to that man."

"If I could get one hour alone with him, thirty minutes even …" Meagan sighed and dropped onto the edge of the bed facing me. "He'd be in heaven and I'd be right there with him."

Such a bold statement coming from me would have been laughable, but coming from Meagan it wasn't so funny. The "sex kitten" of the group, Meagan was beautiful, intelligent, and had never met a man she couldn't bag. I didn't doubt for a second that if Brad Pitt was single and within a twelve mile radius of Meagan, she would have him in her bed in record time.

Katarina stalked to the bed where she'd left her purse. When she returned and crouched in front of me, she was holding a bottle of mascara. "It's not black, it's brown, but it's better than nothing. Open your eyes wide."

As in Star Trek, resistance was futile. Arguing would net me nothing. In the end, I'd be settled before Katarina and submitting to whatever make-up scheme she envisioned for me. It wasn't all bad, though. Katarina was much better with make-up than I was on my best day. She knew how to work colors, how to blend them and bring out my eyes. This was my first real date with Jake and Dev, so I was pretty much willing to undergo any discomfort to ensure I'd look good for them. "How about," Meagan began, "*Thelma and Louise,* Brad?"

"Oh shit!" Ann sat up and began to fan herself. "You're right."

"Was he fine or was he fine?"

"He was damn fine! Oh! And *Troy,* Brad."

Ann nodded. When she turned to face me, I knew it was my turn to add my Brad Pitt flick pick. "I know you're dating two of the sexiest men in Baltimore, but you have to have a favorite."

Lipstick on, I stared up at the ceiling so Katarina could apply eyeliner, something she refused to let me do myself because--according to her--I always made myself look like an ancient Egyptian with a half-inch of kohl under my eyes. "I don't though," I said of Brad. "They go overboard making him look appealing to women in his movies. Take *Troy* for instance. What ancient warrior looked like Brad Pitt did in that movie?"

Ann waved this off. "We don't want a history lesson, Stella, just your favorite Brad. I know you have one. Everyone has one."

"Any woman with a pulse has one," Meagan corrected.

Katarina sat back and examined her handy work. "Okay, all I have to do is blend your eye shadow and line your upper lids with liner, and then you're done."

I closed my eyes, Katarina began to gently rub my lids, and Ann went on. "Come on, Stella. Choose a Brad." She, with the help of Meagan, battered me until they wore me down. As Katarina was sitting back on her heels and pronouncing me done, I got to my feet and blew a gasket. "All right! Yes, I do have a favorite Brad."

"I knew it," Ann announced. "Give it up. Which one is it?"

Throwing caution and common sense to the wind, I announced, "*Kalifornia* Brad."

Immediately, the room went silent. The girls glanced at each other, each looking as though she'd just eaten a sour lemon. Katarina's lip curled, her eyes shifted from Ann then back to me. "*Kalifornia* Brad?" she asked. "You're joking, right?"

"No, I'm not joking," I said, defensive. "What the hell is wrong with *Kalifornia* Brad?"

Meagan, who seemed to be slowly regaining her sense, answered before anyone else could. "He was demented in that movie."

"And he wore dirty clothes and had greasy hair," Katarina added. "And a disgusting beard."

"So what," I said. "Dirty clothes or not, it was still Brad Pitt under there. He was just acting. He wasn't really the character, Early."

"That's so disgusting, Stella."

"Early was just a role," I insisted, wishing I'd kept my mouth shut. "It was still Brad Pitt."

Ann shook her head.

"My mom invited Steven Howard to my birthday dinner," I blurted, desperate to change the subject.

Again, the room went silent.

Ann, who hadn't gone to high school with us, frowned. "What? Should I know who Steven Howard is?"

Katarina shook her head. "No. He was Stella's boyfriend in high school."

Ann swung to face me. "And your mom invited him to your birthday dinner? What about Jake and Dev?"

As if summoned by the mention of their name, my doorbell chimed. "That's what I have to figure out." I started for the door. "Lock up when you leave."

* * * *

8:12 PM

This was our first *real* date. Up until now my time with Jake and Dev--though fun--had been very informal. Let's face it, our get-togethers before tonight had been for sex. Period. But tonight I'd be wined, dined, and romanced … and I couldn't wait.

Jake showed up wearing a crisp, double-breasted, black suit. The purple, button-up shirt would have made any other man look like a pansy, but Jake had the kind of body I was willing to wager could pull off a tutu. He'd gone with a formal tie and had pulled his raven hair back. It was held in place by a plain, suede band.

Running counterpoint to Jake's respectable suit and tie, Dev had appeared on my doorstep in leather pants, a wooly maroon sweater, and ass-kicker boots. In truth, it was difficult to imagine Dev in anything other than leather; the man seemed to live in it. Though I figured if I looked half as good in leather as Dev, I wouldn't wear anything else either. His shoulder length tresses were a rich chocolate brown that hung loose and wild around his shoulders.

Jake pulled my front door shut behind me and placed a gentle hand on my lower back to guide me to the stairs. All the while I wondered when and if I should tell them about my birthday dinner and my birthday dinner guest.

It took us longer than it should have to get to the restaurant. Baltimore's streets were slick with slush so Jake drove slowly, maneuvering around curves with careful precision. The sidewalks were laden with drifts of dirty snow and patches of ice, making walking difficult for those gutsy enough to make their way around the city on foot. As we drove toward Little Italy, I gazed out the window at the pedestrians, marveling at those who'd ventured out wearing little more than thin spring jackets. Even with the heat going full blast inside of the truck I was still chilled to the bone from the walk from my building to the car.

I gazed at the looming buildings as we drove, smiling to myself at how pretty all the glimmering lights within looked against the snowfall. Winter in Baltimore was pretty from this vantage, but I was still looking forward to spring.

We arrived at the restaurant at eight forty-five on the dot. Germano's Trattoria is a stylish Italian bistro in Little Italy. Neither the upstairs or downstairs dining room is very large, but the restaurant has a cozy atmosphere. The muted colors and linen tablecloths give the restaurant a welcoming ambiance that warmed me as soon as I entered.

We'd ordered a bottle of merlot once we were settled. Dev and I were seated side by side, at Jake's request, while Jake had situated himself across the table so he could stare intermittently at us. This was something he did a lot.

Though Jake was behaving as he usually did, Dev didn't seem himself. His eyes were puffy, his pupils rimmed in red as though he'd been crying for the better part of the day. I noticed that he'd brushed his hair so it hung over his face, as though he was trying to hide his eyes. A closer examination proved his skin was paler than usual, and blotchy.

"Stop frowning, Dev," Jake said. "You'll make Stella feel as though you don't want to be here."

Dev sighed, dragged a hand through his waves, then turned to me and attempted to smile. "I'm sorry, kitten. I have a lot on my mind tonight."

In retrospect, I know how stupid and selfish my initial response was to this statement, but I couldn't help it. My first thought was to wonder how on earth he could have anything other than me on his mind tonight. This was our first real date!

Despite my adolescent emotions, I reached for him, gave his thigh a companionable squeeze, and tried to meet his eyes. He looked away, but put a hand over mine and squeezed back. I edged closer to him. "What's wrong?"

He tried to swallow. His Adam's apple bobbed up and down with his struggles.

Jake stood, leaned over the table and clasped the bottle of wine the waitress had brought a few minutes earlier. Wine sloshed into Dev's glass. Jake practically upended the bottle as he poured. He set the flute before Dev and demanded, "Drink."

Dev complied. The entire contents were gone in about five seconds.

Breathing deeply, he returned the empty wineglass to the table then sat back. "Thanks. I needed that."

"What's wrong?" I asked again.

Dev waved the question off. "Oh, it's nothing. Really, I don't know why I'm so shocked. It's nothing new."

"What?" I demanded, and then shifted in my seat until I was face to face with him. "Who hurt you?"

Dev studied me for a moment. "Want to put him in his place, do you? No worries, kitten, I can handle him."

"Him?" All kinds of horrible scenarios flashed in my mind's eye. The preeminent one featured Dev in a back alley being beaten to a bloody pulp by a band of homophobic bastards. Only problem with this was Dev had said, him, singular; not them, plural. Another problem was the fact that, other than his bloodshot eyes and pallor, Dev looked as he usually did. No bruised eyes or split lips. Also, I kind of figured Jake would annihilate any person stupid enough to lay hands on Dev.

So if this wasn't a case of a homophobe attack, what was it? "Who?"

Dev didn't reply at first. He took a sip from his third glass of wine, exchanged a look with Jake and sighed again. "It's not that I'm trying to keep anything from you, kitten. I was hoping to have a nice dinner. I don't want to ruin our night with this."

Jake, looking his most grim, refilled his own wine glass. "Well, I think it's too late for that."

I felt duty bound to rush to Dev's defense. "That's a little harsh, don't you think?"

Jake met my glare. "As a matter of fact, I don't. The son of a bitch doesn't deserve Dev, and he knows it. The bastard certainly doesn't merit having the attention of this meal on him." Jake leaned over the table and hissed, "Fuck him, Dev."

Even if I couldn't see the angry flash in Jake's emerald eyes, I would have known by his inflection that he wasn't talking about sex.

"Come on, Jake," Dev said. "That's not fair."

"Fuck him," Jake said again, then sat back. "Who gives a shit what he thinks."

"He's my father. I care."

"You're almost thirty, Dev. Grow up."

Dev reared back as if struck.

Before Dev could respond, Jake began again. "I'm sorry, but you know how I feel about that man. Why do you let him do this to you?"

Sighing, Dev shrugged and repeated, "He's my father, Jake."

I figured it was time for me to speak up. Jake loved Dev, I knew that, but he was about as gentle as a boar. Dev was in pain. What he needed was to be comforted. On some level he probably wanted to talk about this, get it off his chest.

I pulled my hand free of his and began massaging the soft skin at the back of Dev's neck, trying to soothe the tension from him as best I could. "What did your father do?"

"Shit Stella," Jake said, "let it go."

"He's upset. He needs to talk."

"No. What he needs is to write that man off."

Dev stared at Jake. I wondered if he was debating whether or not to continue the conversation or let it go, as Jake wished. "My sister is getting married in July," he began. "I got the invitation in the mail today." Dev paused, cleared his throat, and then continued. "I have three sisters, Stella. No brothers. I'm the only boy … the only son. The one meant to carry on the family name. When my father found out about me … long story short, he disowned me. I've been *excommunicated* from the family. I haven't been home in nearly two years. My mom and my sisters come to see me here in Baltimore, but the last time I saw my father he told me he never wanted to see my face again."

Jake shoved Dev's wine at him. "Drink. It'll make this easier."

Dev nodded, and emptied the wine from his glass. "Anyway," he began again. "You can imagine what I was thinking when I got the invitation. Will I be welcomed if I go or will my presence turn her wedding into a catastrophe? So I called my sister, Rachel, to see if anything had changed."

"And," I prodded, when he seemed on the verge of stopping.

"And nothing's changed. But Rachel said she and her fiancé want me there. She doesn't care what Dad thinks."

"How do you feel?"

Dev shrugged. "I want to go. Of course I want to go, but I don't want to ruin the wedding. I'm not that selfish."

"What about your sister? She knows your father as well as you do. If she's willing to risk it, shouldn't you?"

"I don't know."

"It's her wedding, after all. Aren't her feelings more important than your father's?"

"That's what I said," Jake interjected.

Dev gazed across the room, his eyes seemed larger and sadder than ever. "Yeah, of course Rachel's feelings are more important."

"I don't have to go," Jake continued. "And I won't be offended if you go alone. I know how things are with your father. Go and enjoy the wedding. You have a right to be there."

Dev shook his head. "It doesn't matter if I go alone or with you. Either way, whenever my dad looks at me he'll see a gay man. He can't stand to be around me, Jake. I know he'll make a scene. I can't do that to Rachel. I won't do that her."

"Then take Stella."

A bit of the wine I'd been sipping slid down the wrong way, sending me into a spasm of coughs.

When the coughing fit subsided, I didn't miss a beat. "I don't think that's a good idea, Jake," I said, wiping stray choke tears away. "If Dev's father doesn't like you, what do you think he'll say about me? You may be a man, but you're white ... sort of." Jake was Native-American and Puerto Rican, not exactly WASP material. "I'm black, Jake. African-American. A minority."

"I noticed," Jake said dryly.

Dev, who'd looked too much like he was contemplating this ridiculous idea, studied me. "I don't know. It may work. My father is a man. I'm sure he'll appreciate your ... attributes. Anyway, he's never been a racist. A homophobe yes, but a racist, no."

Despite the fact that this had been his idea, Jake couldn't keep himself from making a cynical remark. "I bet his best friend is black."

Dev grinned. "No, his best friend is white."

For the first time tonight, Dev was beginning to look like his usual self. I didn't care, though. I wasn't getting roped into this.

"What do you say, Stella," Dev said, looking hopefully at me. "Would you do this for me?"

"What exactly would I have to do?"

"Not much. Just come with me to Virginia. It wouldn't be for more than a few days. Three, maybe four ... five at the most."

"Five days?"

"Come on, kitten. Do this and I'll make it more than worth your while."

I wanted to say no, wanted to refuse, nevertheless I heard myself give in. "Okay. Just let me know how many days when you know for sure so I don't book too many clients for Ann to cover on her own. Late June, early July we get dig notes from an archeological team working in Northern Virginia. We have to get their field notes prepped for publication and it's a lot of work. And there's always a ton or resumes to write. You'd be surprised how clueless people are when it comes to knowing what should and should not go in a resume."

Dev leaned toward me and placed a dry kiss on my lips. "Thank you, Stella."

I didn't get a chance to reply because the waitress appeared with our entrees. She set them on the table before us, moving slower than I thought necessary.

"Would you like extra parmesan on that?" she asked Dev, parmesan dispenser hovering over his plate.

"No, this is good," Dev said.

The waitress pulled her hand back, seemed ready to retreat, then blurted, "Aren't you Cinder, the singer of Maverick? I saw you at Hammerjacks in January and I just think ... well ... you're awesome!"

Dev was the lead singer of Maverick and at the mention of Cinder, his alter ego, he slouched and fixed the requisite grimace to his face. Cinder, as Dev had told me countless times, didn't smile. Smiling ruined the sinister image.

"I am, aren't I," Dev agreed, rather smugly I thought. And either I was losing my mind or his Irish accent was more pronounced than it had been five seconds ago.

The waitress nodded. "You are. I've seen Maverick live eight times and every time you get better."

"Thank you."

"And I've got all your albums. Even the European imports."

"That must have cost you a pretty penny."

She nodded again. "But it was worth it." Her eyes flickered toward me, then back to Dev. "You're amazing," she repeated the pronouncement, this time clutching at her heart like an adolescent at a Justine Timberlake concert. "When's your next album coming out?"

Dev shrugged. "We're on break. Should be back in the studio next month, though."

"I can't wait."

"On pins and needles are you?"

Her head bobbed wildly. I feared she'd give herself whiplash.

"Wish I had one of your CD's with me but I never imagined I'd be serving you tonight. I can't wait to tell my friends."

I exchanged a look with Jake, who was staring at the girl and silently shaking his head. The edge of his lip was quirked into a humorless smile and he was looking at the waitress as though he'd like to do something unpleasant to her.

Probably sensing Jake's annoyance, Dev clasped the waitress's hand, set a kiss on it, and sent her off in a haze of stumbles and giggles. When she was out of view, Dev sat up and grinned. "Sorry about that."

I didn't know what else to do so I shook my head like Jake. "Does that happen to you a lot?"

"Believe me, Stella," said Jake, "you don't want to know."

Dinner was wonderful. The food couldn't have tasted better. The pasta was firm, the sauce spicy without being overwhelming, and the wine delicious. We were having a fantastic night. Jake shared a few anecdotes about his childhood, I spoke of my sisters and my mom--though I didn't mention Steven or the party, and Dev's mood lightened considerably. That's why what happened during dessert came as a complete and total shock.

"Take off your panties and give them to Dev," Jake said, conversationally.

I forced myself to remain silent and wait. Surely this had to be a joke.

"Do it."

"My panties," I whispered. "You want me to take them off?"

Jake gave me one, decisive nod. "Right now."

I felt a brief impulse to demand, *or what,* but that would have been unnecessary. I knew what would happen if I didn't do what was requested of me. I always knew what would happen. The threat had been hanging over my head since I met Dev. If I refused, Jake would let Dev have his way with me. This meant me, backside in the air, with Dev standing over me--whatever implement of punishment he preferred in hand. I could handle Jake with a paddle since he never swatted me too hard, but both men had indicated that Dev would make no such assurances. Dev was a bit of a sadist when it came right down to it. If Jake turned him loose with a paddle I didn't doubt Dev would make sure it hurt.

Instead of arguing, I eased my chair further under the table and pulled the white tablecloth over my lap. I was wearing stockings, thankfully, so I wouldn't have to struggle to free myself of pantyhose. Still, I couldn't decide how I felt about this turn of events.

"You're taking a very long time, Stella," Jake informed me.

I swallowed and nodded my ascent.

As I squirmed out of my panties, I marveled at how quickly dinner had turned from Dev's misery, to friendly conversation, and finally to my submission. I was often left reeling by how quickly, and unexpectedly Jake could exert his dominance. More shocking, though, was how much I enjoyed it. Though I was truly scandalized at the prospect of being sans panties in a public restaurant, the more I thought about it, the more I thrilled I was at the idea. Even as my panties slid down my calves and I reached to clasp them, I knew I'd have a difficult time concentrating on my tiramisu for the remainder of dinner. My body had warmed and begun to tingle. As the seconds ticked by I was becoming light-headed with desire.

I held my panties--Victoria's Secret, thank the stars-- balled in my fist, and placed them in Dev's waiting hand under the table.

"Good girl," Dev purred. "Now spread your legs. Nice and wide."

My face heated and erotic need descended on me. My breath seeped out on a long sigh when Dev placed his hand on my thigh.

My legs trembled and I struggled to obey. I wasn't afraid, but I'd never done anything like this. What if someone saw what we were doing? I'd be horrified.

Dev edged closer, slipped his arm around my waist and pulled me close. "That's it," he soothed into my ear. "Nice and wide."

When I spread my legs as wide as I could without drawing attention to myself, I chanced a look at Jake.

His eyes, hazy with lust, scorched me where I sat. Dragging his tongue over his lower lip, Jake transferred his gaze from me to Dev, and then nodded.

Dev pressed the fingers of his free hand against my clitoris. The pleasure of that simple touch was quick and intense. I had to bite my lip to keep from yelping in surprise. He rubbed me, bringing a surprised gasp from my throat. "You're so wet already, kitten."

This was a fact I was well aware of.

Removing his fingers, Dev turned to Jake and gave him a nearly imperceptible nod.

Jake spooned a bite of tiramisu into his mouth and studied me for a moment. I waited impatiently, wondering if anyone could smell my arousal and praying it wasn't so.

"Ease lower in your chair, Stella," Jake said as he chewed.

Without pausing, I did. "Oh!" I chirped, but remained where I was. "Jake?"

He wiggled what I guessed was his toe against my clit, a wicked grin on his face.

Pleasure oozed over me and a violent shudder shook my body. I had to grab the table to steady myself.

"That feel good, kitten?" Dev asked, lips to my ear.

I gave him a frantic nod.

I had to get control of myself. I scanned the restaurant. Nobody seemed to be watching us, but they would if I made a spectacle.

Jake stroked my clit again, nearly sending me over the edge. Dev's fingers had felt wonderful a moment before, but Jake's toe, sheathed in his dress sock, was like heaven. The rough material felt amazing.

"The last few weeks have been great, Stella," Jake said casually, as though he had no idea what was happening under the table. "Don't you think?"

I didn't want to answer questions. I didn't want to talk. All I wanted to do was close my eyes and lose myself in what Jake was doing to me. Still, I forced myself to nod.

"Dev? Does Stella seem distracted to you? I don't think she's listening to me. What do you think?" His toe froze, mid-rub, and I nearly screamed in protest.

Dev rubbed the nape of my neck, much as I had rubbed his earlier, but for very different reasons. "I think she's listening, but she does seem distracted."

Jake resumed his slow torture, rubbing his toes against my engorged nub and sending a riot of sensations flooding my body. It was such an exquisite pleasure, this secret torment, and I lost myself in the thrill of it.

Dev's lips tickled my ear as he slid closer and began whispering in his rich, baritone voice. "You know what we'd like right now? We'd like to take you out of here, bring you home with us. We'd make you lie in bed between us so we could fuck you senseless. Would you like that, kitten?"

"Yes," I hissed through my teeth.

Jake edged lower in his own seat. Eyes steady on my face, he worked me with his toes. Stroking my clit in languorous circles that were near to sending me over the edge. I clutched at the edge of the table again, gripped the wood and cloth tighter as Jake continued.

"Cum for me Stella," Jake mouthed.

As though he controlled the very functions of my body, the damn broke and a powerful orgasm rippled through me. I gasped at the force of it, had to bite my tongue to staunch a cry of pure joy. The sensations came at me in waves, thundering over me so forcefully that Dev had to wrap his arms around me to keep me from tumbling off my chair.

I have no idea how much time passed before I was able to think a coherent thought again. But as the pleasure slowly receded, I realized Jake was watching me from across the table, smiling.

"Can we have our check, please?" he asked our star struck waitress when she returned to our table. "We have to get home."

Chapter Three

11:01 PM

I sat at the foot of the bed, gazing into the fireplace in Jake and Dev's bedroom, trying to figure out where they'd gone. I looked around me, took in the warm green and muted maroon hues of the room and tried to relax. They'd left me on their massive four-poster bed, the sheer curtains spread wide so I could sit with my legs dangling off the side, not quite touching the floor. They'd left me in there nearly twenty minutes ago. What could be taking them so long?

Clearly they were up to something.

"Stella," Jake said, pulling me from my silent musings.

I looked up and nearly swallowed my tongue. Instantly I sat erect, and stared in admiration. Jake looked amazing. There was something indescribably sexy about the tilt of his head and the full line of his lips. I couldn't tell exactly what he was wearing, but it looked sort of like a jet-black, wet suit. It sheathed his body like a second skin, so deliciously tight I could make out every bulge and curve on him. His hair was loose, nearly unkempt in the way it flowed in unruly waves down his back. He was wearing boots, a pair of knee-high ass-kicker boots that made an already sinfully sexy outfit look downright lethal. "What are you wearing?" I asked, breathlessly.

Jake advanced into the room and came to stand beside the bed. Setting large hands on his hips, he surveyed me. There was an eager gleam in his eyes, a feral hunger in the way he looked at me that had my heart racing.

"Did you enjoy yourself tonight?" he asked, completely ignoring my question.

Too busy gawking to respond verbally, I nodded.

"Good. And the food?"

I had time to offer a single nod, and then Dev appeared. Instantly I knew they had something fun planned.

I didn't know where on Dev to settle my greedy eyes first. Every inch of him was delectably perfect. Donning a body suit similar to Jake's, Dev's lithe body was just as enticing in the form-fitting suit as was Jake's. Though instead of ass-kicker boots, Dev wore thigh-high boots with elaborate silver buckles and fastenings. His hair was smoothed away from his face and clasped tightly at the nape of his neck. The overall affect was slightly menacing. He looked severe, nearly military, and extremely sexy.

I felt the air spill out of me on a sigh. Lust would have driven me to my knees had I been standing.

"Come here," Jake said, motioning to a spot on the floor directly between them.

"You both look amazing. What's the occasion?"

"Come here, Stella,"

I wet my tongue and swallowed. Careful the lust racing through my body didn't make me keel over, I got to my feet, then stumbled forward a step. Getting another, longer look at them as they stood side-by-side, I sighed yet again.

Eventually, I made my way to the spot Jake had indicated. Standing so close to them made me feel faint.

Dev took a step toward me, brushed his lips against my cheek. "Good girl."

I swallowed and strove for calm. I didn't have a clue what they were up to, but I knew from experience the best thing I could do was follow directions.

Folding his arms imperiously over his chest, Jake continued to gaze at me. "Do you want to know what we're going to do to you, Stella?"

My face heated as another, more powerful rush of lust surged inside of me. I nodded.

"First we're going to make you take off your clothes. I want you naked. Then we're gonna show you who that sexy little body belongs to."

My stomach clenched. I would never be able to explain to myself why such domineering talk always turned me on.

Dev fingered a strap of my dress and then gave it a gentle tug. "I bet you'd like that. And I'll bet she already knows who she belongs to. Don't you, kitten?"

I nodded.

"Don't you?" Dev said, louder. There was a hint of steel in his voice that sent a shiver of anticipation through me. "Answer me."

I opened my mouth and was surprised by the squeak that came forth. "Yes."

Jake brushed the tips of his fingers down my spine and leaned in close so he could whisper in my ear. "Who do you belong to?"

Crap! They wanted me to say it ... out loud! I couldn't actually say it. I could think it, maybe pantomime it, but saying it when I wasn't busy having an orgasm? That was too much.

I stared at Dev, hoping he'd see by my wide, pleading eyes that this was beyond me. Unfortunately, Dev began tapping his toe impatiently. "Say it, beautiful. Tell us who your Masters are."

Masters? When had we decided to use that word?

I licked my lips, closed my eyes ...

"Open your eyes and look at us."

I opened them, and then cleared my throat. "I belong," I began, then stalled. "To you," I exhaled, "and Jake."

"Every inch of you," Jake said, coming up close behind me just as Dev was praising me with a "Good girl."

I stood still as stone, unsure of how I was supposed to react. To say I'd never been in this situation before was the understatement of the year.

"Take your clothes off Stella," Jake said and stepped away from me.

Dev stepped away as well. Neither went far, and both continued to watch me.

Getting out of my dress wasn't difficult. It was only a matter of unzipping and letting the garment slide the length of my body to the floor. I stepped out of my heels and lost a good two inches of height. Getting out of the stockings took a little longer, but in minutes I was naked, save the rings on my fingers and the necklace at my throat.

Watching me like a hawk, Jake smiled. "Very good. Now sit on the bed and show your Master's their pussy."

"Do what?"

"Sit on the bed," Dev repeated, slowly enunciating each word. "Then spread your thighs so we can see our pussy."

I swallowed. Hard. It felt like something very large was caught in my throat. "You want me to do that now?"

"Right now."

What was the big deal, I asked myself? I was dating two men, after all. I couldn't walk to the bed and spread my legs?

Aroused, nervous, and unsure of myself, I went to the bed and settled atop the downy comforter. It was soft as cotton beneath me. It was like sitting on a band of fluffy clouds.

Though my legs hung rigidly, I'd decided to do as they said. They hadn't steered me wrong yet, so I trusted them.

Forcing fear from my mind, I spread my thighs wide.

One of them--I didn't know which since I was staring at my feet--let out a slow breath.

"Good girl." That was Dev. "Isn't she beautiful?"

"I have impeccable taste."

I could hear the muffled sound of boots against carpet as they approached.

"Speaking of taste--" Dev began. His face came into my line of vision when he crouched before me. "I want you to scoot further back on the bed."

I met Dev's gaze. Was he about to do *it* to me? I wasn't sure if I could handle having his mouth on me. "Dev--"

Dev shook his head. "Come on, kitten. Don't be shy."

The bed dipped and I nearly jumped out of my skin. I'd been so focused on Dev I'd momentarily forgotten about Jake. I stiffened at the touch of his hands on my waist, nearly cried out when he lifted me and brought me to the center of the bed.

Jake kneeled behind me, knees pressed to my hips with his chest flush against my back. I thought I'd melt into his warmth. Even encased in rubber, Jake's body felt amazing.

"Relax, Stella," Jake said into my ear. "You'll enjoy this. I promise."

Again, I marveled at what was about to happen, at what I thought Dev was about to do.

"I want the taste of you in my mouth," Dev said, as if reading my mind. He climbed onto the bed, the buckles on his boots jangling as he moved, and sprawled between my spread legs. "I want to feel your pussy on my tongue. So be a good girl and open wide."

I did as told, shuddering under the weight of anticipation.

When Dev kissed my inner thigh, I sighed. When he ran his tongue over my skin, I cried out. Hot air peppered my sex as he trailed a path with his tongue up my inner thigh. Delicious sensations thrummed through my body.

"Ready kitten?" Dev asked.

Jake wrapped his arms around me and pulled me so close that I could feel his every inhalation as though they were my own. He began to play with my nipples, squeezing the erect nubs between his fingers and tickling them with the pads of his thumbs. The torture was wonderful. His breath was hot on the back of my neck, his tongue was wet and knowing as he nibbled on my lobe. "If we hurt you or scare you," Jake said, dipping his tongue into my ear, "tell us and we'll stop. Understand?"

I gave him a wild nod.

He moaned.

So slowly I wanted to scream, Dev cupped my bottom and breathed against my glistening slit. "You smell wonderful, kitten."

When I felt his tongue, I would have screamed if Jake hadn't drawn my head back and captured my lips in a kiss. Even as Jake's mouth moved lusciously over mine, he captured my wrists and pressed them to my lower back so they were pinioned between our bodies.

Dev ran his tongue over the sensitive folds of my nether lips and skimmed my skin with leisurely strokes that set my blood to boil. More hot air pepper me as Dev breathed, his nose inadvertently pressed against my clit as he delved deeper. My clitoris seized at the contact, my back arched in reaction to the delectable sensation.

My entire body vibrated beneath this luscious onslaught; I quivered.

Jake deepened our kiss and held me immobile. "You're our prisoner now, Stella," Jake whispered against my eager lips. "And we're never letting you go." He applied pressure to my wrists, demonstrating just how tightly he was going to hold on to me. Even as the bones in my arms were pressed together, I moaned under the sensual delight of belonging to two such extraordinary men.

Jake captured my mouth for another taste as Dev's tongue was sinking into my depths. Dev lapped my cream into his mouth like a starving man. "Kitten, you taste so good."

Desperate for more of this, I writhed between them. The sensation of having both mouths on me, savoring me, was nearly too much. When, a moment later, Dev found my clit with his tongue and closed his mouth over it, I saw stars. I released a strangled cry and closed my eyes against the barrage of sensations coursing through me. Then he sucked the engorged nub into his mouth and began licking in earnest.

Of its own accord, my body spasmed--not in orgasm but in sheer pleasure. I bucked and twisted, fought to remain silent as Dev suckled harder. My body was pure sensation. Every touch was ecstasy; every lick had me swallowing down a whimper.

On the very edge of control, on the periphery of climax, Jake--the son of a bitch--pulled away from me and said, "That's enough Dev. She's about to cum."

A small cry of protest spilled from between my lips.

I watched in shocked outrage as Dev reared up on all fours. His rubber suit bulged at his biceps when he began to crawl toward me. His mouth glistened with my juice and his lips were split with a self-satisfied smirk. "Poor baby," he said, not meaning a word. "Were you about to climax?"

"You know I was."

"Patience is a virtue, Stella," Jake advised. "Anyone ever tell you that?"

I would have made a caustic reply, but at that moment I was pressed backward into the downy bedspread. Suddenly on my back, I stared up at the ceiling in surprise.

Like bookends, both men eased down on either side of me. For a moment, they gazed like hungry lions at each other. Then the moment passed, and they refocused on me.

Dev ran his fingers over my stomach, his touch so light it tickled. Though there wasn't anything particularly erotic about what he was doing, my skin felt like it was coming alive beneath his touch. He fingered my belly, traced a path to my breasts, and then began to gently squeeze my engorged nipples. "That feel good, baby?" Dev asked.

I began to answer, but my words ended on a sigh. Jake set his hand between my legs and curled his fingers until one slid easily inside of me. Gliding a second finger within, he curved them and tickled.

I threw my head back and cried out. The sense that I was floating on the air, adrift on a plain of existence where sensation was all there was nearly overwhelmed me.

"That's it," Jake crooned. "Relax for us. Feel that?"

He tickled me again and I thought I'd lose my mind. Another spasm shook me and I arched in surprise.

Hell, yeah, I felt that.

"That's your G-spot." He moved his fingers again, showing me for a third time that he knew exactly what he was doing. "Feel good?"

"Yes!"

As Jake continued his exotic manipulations of my body, Dev fell on me. His lips were soft, yet demanding; sweet as honey, but determined. Our lips locked and our tongues entwined. Though I could taste myself on him I didn't want to pull back.

I moaned into his mouth, tangled my fingers in his hair and pulled him closer. I needed more of him, more of what both men were giving me. My body was on fire, I was overcome from the sheer bliss of what was happening to me.

"Oh yeah," I murmured against his lips, "I'm about--" I let out a cry of protest when Dev's lips left mine. But even as I opened my mouth to complain, Jake slid his fingers free of me. "No!"

Sucking both fingers into his mouth, Jake regarded me. "You cum when we're ready for you to cum. Not before."

"But that felt good." I sought comfort in Dev's eyes, but found nothing but amusement.

"Poor baby," he said. "We're so cruel to you, aren't we?"

"Yes," I agreed. "You are."

"It's not as bad as all that," he said, rolling fully on top of me. He reached into a flap at the crotch of his rubber suit and pulled his erect cock free. "Is it?" He parted my legs with his thigh and froze, poised at my entrance. "Well, is it?"

Eager for him to continue, I shook my head. "No. You're both wonderful."

"Good girl."

He drove into me with one smooth thrust.

Ecstasy descended on me with earth shattering force. My insides felt hot and slick as he withdrew and drove himself home a second time. "I'm gonna fuck you so good," he promised against my lips, matching words to action as he spoke.

I gripped the bed sheets in both hands and held on for dear life. I was driven toward the headboard with every penetration despite my handhold on the bed. The comforter was soft as silk beneath me, gentle against my skin as Dev drove me along its length with every possession.

Jake's erect penis bobbed into view. He was so excited that the head of his cock seemed twice its normal size.

Without question, Dev's lips parted and encircled Jake's cock. Wet, slurping sounds seeped from his lips as he worked to swallow Jake.

I gasped. I'd never seen them do this before. Dev was giving Jake head! Right in front of me.

Jake loomed over us, crouching on his knees with closed eyes as he lost himself to Dev's ministrations. A moment later, though, Jake grasped Dev by the hair and tugged gently, releasing his cock from Dev's lips. "I want both of you to suck me."

Dev didn't need any further prodding. As Jake bent over me, erection bobbing in my face, Dev ran his tongue along the shaft. He seemed starved for this, so hungry for Jake's cock I wondered briefly if there really was a question who was Dom and who was sub in this relationship. Clearly Jake wore the pants.

"Suck me, Stella," Jake whispered. "I want to feel your mouth, both of your mouths on me. Worship my dick with your tongues."

As Jake spoke, Dev thrust hard, rotated his hips, and released Jake long enough to grin down at me when I moaned. He slipped a hand beneath my head, cradling it as he lifted. I found in this position my lips were pressed firmly to Jake's cock, leaving me no choice but to comply with Jake's request.

Dev rocked inside of me and I darted my tongue out, let it glide over the surface of Jake's skin.

Jake pumped his hips. "More."

Careful to keep my teeth tucked under my lips, I nibbled him. His hips bucked in response, making my tongue glide over his hardness. When I licked the hot flesh, he let out a small sigh. So I licked faster, found that if I licked his cockhead my tongue came into direct contact with Dev's. When our tongues touched, a shudder ran through my body. We lapped at each other for luscious moments, and then returned our attention to Jake.

Dev continued his merciless possession of me. Driving into me so hard and fast, my toes curled. I could feel his thrusts in my stomach, and the delicious sensations all over.

"That's enough, Dev," Jake said, panting. He eased back and out of our reach. They locked eyes, then without question, Dev levered himself up until he was crouching between my thighs, his hips rocking continually against me.

"Dev fucking you good, baby?" Jake asked, staring down at me.

Dev drew back and descended again, sending my body into ripples of pure rapture. Even as he withdrew, my stomach trembled. My sex clenched and I could feel something powerful uncoiling inside of me.

Dev clasped my ankles and hoisted them to his shoulders, changing the angle so every penetration was deeper than before.

"I know that feels good," Dev told Jake. "Doesn't it kitten?"

I couldn't answer. My body bucked of its own accord, trembled every time Dev drove in me. My head rocked back and forth and I cried out, desperate for release.

"I'll have to try that on you later," Jake said, eyes devouring me as he spoke to Dev. "She's losing her mind."

"How 'bout I do it to you? Nothing wrong with being fucked when it feels that good. Isn't that right, kitten?"

He drove deep and pulsed, doubling the sensations descending on me. No longer able to control myself, I screamed. When that did nothing to ease the tension, I forced a fist into my mouth and bit down.

"Ease back, Dev. I don't want her to cum yet."

Though Dev curled his lip and looked mutinous, he drew back and slowed his thrusts. The pleasure eased to a far more manageable level, and I cried out in adamant protest. "No, Dev. Don't stop. Please."

"I love it when you beg," Dev said, grinning wickedly. "Now tell me how much you love my dick."

I was positively crazed with the need for release, desperate for completion. "I love your dick, Dev. Please, do me harder."

Dev looked at Jake, eyebrow raised.

Jake refocused his attention on me. Eyes simmering with lust, he straddled me, then pressed his bobbing cock to my lips. "You don't cum, until I cum. Understand?"

This had to be a joke. How on earth could I concentrate on Jake when Dev was making me feel so wonderful? Already I was near tears with my need for release. I didn't think I could hold back much longer.

"Can't I have just one itty bitty orgasm?"

Jake gave me a disapproving frown. "You cum before I give you permission and the next time we fuck you will be a month from now."

Now he was being cruel. Nevertheless, I didn't see that I had a choice. "I won't."

"Better not." Saying this, Jake slid into my mouth. "Swallow me, Stella," he murmured. "Every inch."

I felt his huge cockhead glide over my tongue and knew if I didn't swallow I was likely to gag. I spread my mouth in welcome, swallowed until I could feel him deep in the back of my throat.

"That's a good girl," Jake said, approvingly. "Does your Master's dick taste good?"

I nodded and groaned. Even as the tension built inside me, the need of release becoming a constant throb, I gloried in every new sensation. The feeling of being filled by both men at the same time was nearly too much, as was the press of Jake's rubber-clad thighs against my shoulders as he slid deeper into the warmth of my mouth.

I lay on my back, overcome by my need to submit sexually to these men who'd become my lovers. The visual pleasure of Jake's complete dominance sent a bone-deep thrill through me. Even as I stared adoringly at him, he clasped me at the wrists and pinioned my hands to the bed over my head. I had to fight to maintain my equilibrium as a fresh wave of erotic helplessness descended on me.

Jake withdrew from my mouth, eyes pinning me as thoroughly as his body was. "You love this, don't you?"

A desperate sigh wheezed from between my compressed lips.

"Slower, Dev. She's a dominance junkie. Touch her clit and she'll explode."

Before Jake finished talking, Dev slowed the pace. He rocked against me slow, slid easily within my depths then glided out.

Despite the fact that he was doing his damnedest to prolong this experience, I doubted it would help. Jake slid into my mouth as Dev plunged deep. The movements were so perfect, felt so good I nearly climaxed. But I fought against the urge, wrestled against my need to simply let go.

Jake thrust hard and fast, eager for satisfaction. I didn't doubt he was well aware that no matter how hard I tried, I couldn't hold on much longer. Compounding the problem, though Dev had initially slowed his pace, gradually his thrusts were becoming deeper, his breathing less controlled. He heaved a sigh with every penetration, sucked in air as he withdrew. His moans matched my own in volume, if not intensity.

He loosed my ankles and wrapped his arms around my knees, clenching my legs to his body as he drove deeper, thrust harder.

I cried out as the sensation built and my orgasm danced closer. I would have been rocked back by the force of Dev's thrusts if Jake's weight wasn't anchoring me to the bed.

Seeming to sense Dev's struggle for control, Jake released my arms, twisted his torso so he could face Dev, then clasped Dev by the hair, dragging him roughly forward.

Like a man starved for sustenance, Dev sucked Jake's waiting tongue into his mouth. He moaned against Jake's lips while he thrust into me, tasting Jake even as he pounded an erotic cadence into my very core.

"Have to cum," he breathed into Jake. "Let me cum, Jake. This is so fucking good. I can't wait."

Jake released Dev and turned his attention to me.

Nails digging into his knees, teeth planted firmly against my lips, I was doing everything I could to hold off my release.

The only one of us still functioning like a reasoning human being was Jake. He took hold of my arms and pinned them to the bed again. Though his eyes were glassy with what I took to be desire and his lips trembled when he spoke, Jake maintained iron control over himself.

"I'm going to let Dev cum," he said calmly, "but that doesn't mean anything's changed for you. You don't until I do."

The air hiccupped from Dev when Jake plunged into my mouth and said, "Let go, Dev."

With a series of low moans and savage grunts, Dev thrust fast and hard as a piston. Fire danced along my vaginal channel as sensations came at me double time. He growled through every possession, groaned every time he drew back.

With a primal roar, Dev climaxed. At the same moment, Jake spilled creamy cum into my mouth. I lapped at it like a greedy kitten, swallowed every drop.

I compressed my lips against Jake's cock as something decadent uncoiled inside of me. The heat that had been forming within, the sensations that had been threatening all night, released. The climax that had been dancing just out of reach descended on me with such force that I nearly bucked Jake off of me.

Orgasm churned, the delicious thrill of completion settling on me so thoroughly I wanted to cry. I rocked beneath the force, struggled against Dev's iron grip as he gritted out his own completion.

Only when I returned to earth did I realize Jake hadn't given me the order to climax.

Chapter Four

Journal Entry 3/9/05, 2:27 AM

Though the fire in the hearth was dying, it still provided enough light for me to see by. I was lying in the crook of Dev's body. His thigh was tangled with mine, but his fingers were laced with Jake's. Jake lay in front of me, eyes wide and staring.

Sometime after we'd gone to bed I'd begun to think of Dev's dilemma again. I felt horrible for Dev. I couldn't believe a father would disown his own child. Though I had agreed to attend the wedding under duress, the idea of standing at Dev's side when he went to Virginia was beginning to hold more appeal for me. Even if things went well, he'd need emotional support. Seeing his father again after so many years was bound to bring a myriad of unsettling emotions rushing to the surface. Dev was human after all, and bound by the same human emotions that governed all of us.

My mother might be overbearing, but she'd never disown me. She may annoy me, but her annoying behavior came from love.

The more I thought about it, the more pleased I was that they'd thought me an adequate alternative to Jake.

"Stella?"

Pulled from my thoughts, I gazed into Jake's emerald eyes. "Yeah?"

"Two things. First, have you been seeing anyone other than me and Dev?"

The question caught me so off guard that I gasped. Seeing anyone other than them? The question would have been laughable in the extreme if not for the fact that my mother had invited Steven to the house for my birthday. But I hadn't invited him, surely that counted for something. "When would I have the time? Between work and the two of you I've spent the last few weeks exhausted."

Behind me, Dev chuckled. "Good."

Jake levered himself on an elbow. I knew something bad was coming.

"But?" I prodded.

"No buts about it--" Jake said and then paused to chuckle.

"Well," Dev said, laughing, "I wouldn't say *no* buts about it."

This seemed to further amuse Jake. "I was saying, adding a female to our relationship has proven to be a good idea. But we have a problem."

"Problem?" I repeated.

Jake nodded. "The problem is that Dev and I don't like taking turns."

"Taking turns?" Did he mean sex? I loved them taking turns. I lived for them taking turns. I'd never had so many orgasms in my life. If they were about to tell me they'd come up with some idiotic plan--

Jake leaned over me, eyes dark with unspoken promises. "We want to fuck you together. At the same time."

I stared, unsure if I'd heard correctly. How on earth did they think they could have sex with me at the same time? Well, when I sucked on one while the other was inside of me … but we'd done that tonight. The only other thing was … Hell, no!

In an effort to assure himself I understood what he wanted, Jake leaned closer and continued in a husky voice. "I want to bend you over my bed, Stella. Then I want to ease my dick in that virgin ass of yours and take you until you beg me for mercy." Jake gazed at Dev, a slight grin touching the edges of his lips. "Understand, Stella?"

I didn't respond. I was too stunned.

"After I think you're accustomed to having that ass fucked, Dev and I want to take you together. At the same time."

"You wanna put it where?" I asked, hoping against hope I'd misunderstood.

"I think you heard me."

So I had.

Suddenly, I wanted desperately to be inside my cozy home, curled in my own bed. I sat up. "Are you crazy?"

Jake shook his head. "It's perfectly normal."

I thought about making a mad dash for the door, but figured I'd look ridiculous. Also, I didn't want to end my relationship with Jake and Dev, I simply wasn't up for anal intercourse. So I subsided into Dev's warmth and glared at Jake. "Hell, no!"

Dev gave me a peck on the back of my head and drew me deeper into his embrace. "Relax Stella. We won't force you. We want you to enjoy it, not be terrorized by it. You know we'd never do anything to you that didn't feel good, don't you?"

I felt a pout coming on. "I guess. At least you haven't so far."

"So trust us."

"But I've never done *that* before."

"Just think about it, kitten. Try to imagine how good it would feel to lay between us, our focus entirely on making you feel good. I promise you, you'll love it."

Okay, when he put it like that maybe it wouldn't be so bad. Still, this was too big a thing to decide without a lot of thought. This was the kind of thing that required much reflection, deliberation, and consideration on my part. It was also major enough to merit an emergency meeting with the girls. "Can I think about it?"

Jake and Dev exchanged a look. Jake's lips were set in a thin line and his jaw was clenched so tight that, for a moment, I thought he'd say no. But instead of refusing he nodded.

"Think about it, kitten," Dev said. "I promise that you'll love it."

Jake reclined in bed, his eyes remained open. "Another thing, Stella. I told you not to climax until I gave you permission."

Crap! Not this again. "Sex typically leads to orgasm. If you didn't want me to have an orgasm, you shouldn't have spent half the night arousing me."

"You *chose* not to listen, therefore I've no choice but to enforce--"

I sat up again. "One month! You've got to be kidding."

"I'm not through. One month, Stella. Understand Dev? Stella is off-limits for both of us. That means no penetration, no oral sex, no masturbation--"

He continued to tick off a long list of things they wouldn't do to me. Seemed the only thing that was permissible was watching movies together, eating, and talking. "You're crazy, Jake!"

Jake peered at me. "Of course you can get out of your punishment if you agree to accompany Dev and me to a--"

"Party," Dev said into my ear, finishing Jake's thought after Jake trailed off.

"That's right," Jake agreed. "A party. A masquerade ball at a close friend's house."

I regarded Jake with suspicion. His grin widened into a sensual smile, his eyes were luminescent in the firelight, and his bare flesh was warm against me. "If you wanted me to go with you to this party, why didn't you just ask?"

Jake shrugged. "It was more fun this way. You should have seen the look on your face when I said we wouldn't have sex with you for a month."

Dev kissed the edge of my ear. "So will you go with us, kitten?"

Sex was back on the menu and they wanted me to go to a ball. Seemed like a win-win situation to me. "Sure I'll go. Sounds like fun. I've never been to a masquerade ball before."

"Oh, then you'll love this one."

"It's on a Friday in April. The eighth. Are you free that night?"

A week before my birthday. Turns out I was.

Chapter Five

Journal entry 3/10/05, 9:23 AM

Crap! Did I agree to have anal sex with Jake and Dev?

* * * *

11:04 AM

Maybe anal sex won't be that bad. Women have anal sex all the time and manage to live through it. I hear some even enjoy it. Hell, what's the big deal? All I need to do is remember that I'm a sexual pioneer, the amorous equivalent to Christopher Columbus, charting new territory and conquering foreign lands.

* * * *

1:27 PM

Huh, did Christopher Columbus actually "conquer" anything?

* * * *

3:21 PM

Who am I kidding? I don't want to have anal sex.

* * * *

Journal Entry 3/11/05, 2:27 AM

I can't sleep. Visions of incontinence and other horrors that may occur after having anal sex are running rampant in my head.

* * * *

10:51 PM

Since I'm seriously considering this anal thing I need some expert advice. Out of Ann, Katarina, and Meagan, Ann and Meagan are the most likely to know about anal sex. Out of Ann and Meagan, Ann is the most supportive of my relationship with Jake and Dev. Hmm. Must talk with Ann about this. Damn, and she's working at her own house again tomorrow. I must remember to call her in the morning and ask her to come over. The situation has reached critical levels.

* * * *

Journal Entry 3/12/05, 9:27 AM

"I thought you were enjoying Jake and Dev," Ann said into the phone.

"I am, but I need you to come over. We have to talk."

"Why? What'd they do?"

"Can't talk about it over the phone. Just come over. I'll tell you what's up when you get here."

"Should I call the girls?"

I considered the offer, thought about the seriousness of the situation. Anal sex! Katarina and Meagan might not love the fact that I was in a ménage, but if there was ever I time I needed my friends, it was now. "Yes. Call them. We'll meet at my place."

"Actually, why don't we meet at Katarina's? I take it she hasn't called you yet?"

Ann was the first person I'd spoken to this morning and I told her as much.

"Here's the deal. Katarina says we never go to her place so she wants us to come over and watch movies."

I shrugged. "Oh well, guess I'll see you at Katarina's."

* * * *

5:51 PM

"Anal sex isn't funny!" I stomped my foot to emphasize the point. "Not even a little. What should I do?"

We were sitting in Katarina's living room, trying not to go blind from all the white surrounding us. White sofa and loveseat, white walls, white carpet, the only things that weren't white were the two morbid Van Gogh fakes on her walls and the large picture window that looked out onto the Fells Point harbor. Though it was dark outside, from my perch in the living room I could see the bright, neon lights of the Domino building across the water, spelling the company name in large red letters. I knew if I went to the glass, pressed my face against the surface and looked down I'd see people milling around the sidewalk, walking to one of the myriad bars or restaurants in the neighborhood. As usual, I'd wonder if I should have moved to Fells Point, the party district, instead of Mount Vernon, the artsy fartsy district.

Ann lifted her head from the arm of the sofa and gave me a once over. "First thing, stay the hell away from prunes."

Meagan and Ann erupted in laughter, yet again.

I gave Meagan an elbow to the ribs. "Anyone have any usable advice here?"

Katarina, hovering in the corner of the sofa beside Ann, had seemed to close in on herself once I'd told them what the emergency was. Her face had taken on a sickly pale hue and she emitted a sort of groaning, gasping sound every time I said the word anal.

I glanced at her to see if she had anything to add to the discussion. When she shivered, I took that to mean she didn't.

"Well how do you feel about them, Stella?" Meagan wanted to know.

"You wanna know how I feel about Jake and Dev? I like them. A lot."

"Do you trust them?"

I considered. They'd never done anything to make me feel threatened or unsafe. We played a lot of sex games, but neither had ever forced me to do anything I didn't want to. I supposed I did trust them. When it got right down to it, if I didn't trust them I'd never have been able to do all the things I'd done with them thus far. "Yeah, I guess I do."

"So, what's the problem?"

"Pain," a wavering voice said. "Gut wrenching, agonizing, pain. And you can't look very lady-like with your butt in the air. It's undignified."

We all stared at Katarina.

"I'm not worried about looking like a lady," I said. "But pain is a consideration. Won't it hurt?"

Meagan slid her heels off and curled her legs under her black dress slacks. "Not if they do it right."

"You've had anal sex before?"

"Of course. It's not that big a deal. You just have to make sure if you do this, you're in the right frame of mind. You have to want it, otherwise it will hurt."

Ann nodded. "Yeah. Remember to push out against the dick when whoever's fucking you sticks it in. And relax or it'll hurt like a mother."

"Gee, thanks," I said.

"Know what you need?" Ann got to her feet and padded, barefoot, down the hall toward Katarina's office.

I was fast on her heels. If she knew a way to make anal sex feel good, I was all about finding out everything I could.

Katarina's office was tucked in a corner of her fifth-floor condo. A swank white, beige, and mint green area rug had been thrown artfully on the floor. The beige hues brought out the rich tones of her ultra chic credenza and desk. Her laptop, centered to within an inch of its life on the desk, was fluorescent green. A soft, electronic hum of life was rising from it.

Ann settled at the desk. Since Katarina's computer was already on she double clicked the Explorer icon on the desktop.

I stood over her, staring at the screen as Explorer came up and Ann brought up the Yahoo search engine.

"Butt plug?" Katarina read over my shoulder as Ann typed. We exchanged a look.

"Good idea." Meagan slid onto an edge of the desk.

"What we'll do is order one of these for you to practice with, Stella," Ann said. "What size do you think, Meagan?" Ann tilted the screen back so Meagan could have a better view.

Meagan studied the screen with rapt interest.

A series of colorful, pyramid shaped phalluses were lined up on the screen. There were red ones, brown ones, hot pink ones, peach ones, white ones. "What are those for?" I wanted to know.

"Nothing too big," Meagan advised.

"Remember, this has to prepare her for a dick." Ann eyed me. "How big is Jake?"

"What?" I flinched. I'm not a prude, but I sort of think it's inappropriate for my friend to ask me how big my boyfriend's penis is. "He's nice sized."

"Dev?" At my open-mouthed astonishment, she explained. "We have to know what size to get."

Katarina lifted a manicured finger and pointed stiffly at the screen. "Stella's supposed to stick one of those things up her butt?"

Sighing heavily, Ann said, "Yes."

"I'm not sticking a--"

"Butt plug," Ann supplied.

"Butt plug up my butt. Ick! Who sticks plugs up their butt?"

"Either you want to have anal sex or you don't."

"Crap!" I indicated a phallus then retrieved a credit card from my purse.

Still gazing at the plug I selected, Meagan asked, "Jake or Dev? Damn! I'm impressed."

"Eat your heart out."

Ann completed the order then turned to face me. "Just remember Stella, relax and all will go well. Relax and it feels pretty good."

With a look of pure disgust, Katarina looked Ann over. "You like anal sex. Why doesn't that surprise me?"

"Maybe because I'm not a prude like some people."

"I'm no prude. I'll have you know Jim and I have been discussing the pros and cons of exhibitionism. I think we're gonna have sex at Power Plant Live this weekend. I bet even you've never done anything like that before, Ann."

The room went silent.

"You're what?" I demanded.

"Gonna have sex at Power Plant Live this weekend. We've been planning this for a few weeks. This is the first time we're trying something like this so we want to make it exciting."

Power Plant Live was an indoor/outdoor, multi-level nightlife complex built into a courtyard in the heart of Baltimore's tourist district. There were at least five different dance clubs within the complex, countless bars, an outdoor pavilion, restaurants, and a massive live entertainment venue. A huge sign hovered above the area proclaiming, "Power Plant Live" in huge white lights. Once upon a time I considered it one of the coolest places in the city. But even if I felt the same way about it now it was not someplace I'd go for an erotic encounter. "Are you crazy? Don't have sex there."

Meagan grimaced. "Where exactly in Power Plant, pray tell, do you plan to have this little rendezvous?"

Katarina shrugged, as though this was a minor detail. "Either against a corner wall in Have a Nice Day Café or in Bar Baltimore."

Ann, Meagan, and I exchanged horrified glances.

"Please Katarina," Meagan begged, "don't do that. At least not at either of those places. Not around all those twenty-something's."

"We've already decided," Katarina insisted.

I would not allow my friend to do something as ridiculous as going to Power Plant Live to have sex in one of its nightclubs. "Something like this should be done someplace nice. We haven't been to Power Plant Live in years because all the rowdy college kids. You don't want to have sex there." Somehow, turning thirty had changed us in ways we'd never imagined. Places we used to go on the weekend suddenly seemed adolescent and beneath us. Almost overnight we'd gone from frequenting places like Have a Nice Day Café to having drinks at The Oak Room, the upscale lounge where we were paying five hundred friggin' dollars a month for a VIP table.

"There's no place else we can go where we can get away with it," Katarina complained. "And I want to do this. I want to have non-vanilla sex for once in my life. Ann's right. My sex life has been nothing but missionary position after missionary position." She shrugged. "With Jim I feel like I can finally experiment with sex. I never felt so open with a man before."

Meagan stood and walked behind the desk. "Okay then. Since you're determined to do this, have you thought about places outside of Baltimore?"

"Well, no."

"That's your problem. There are plenty of places you can do this. Just because its exhibitionism doesn't mean you have to go trashy. Rent a chalet at the Pocono's then go into the forest and make love. That would be exciting and romantic."

"And no twenty-something shitheads to ruin the mood," Ann added.

"How about," I began, getting into the spirit, "you and Jim take a weekend trip to Colorado. A ski trip. You can drink hot chocolate, cozy up next to a fire, then hit the slopes and find a picturesque spot to make love."

Katarina shook her head. "I love the idea of skiing, but I hate the cold. And this time of year, it's freezing. How about someplace warm?"

"Like the beach?" Ann asked.

Katarina nodded. "Yeah. If we go far enough south the weather will be a lot nicer than it is here."

"Myrtle Beach?"

Meagan shook her head. "Too many teenagers go there. But the Outer Banks would be perfect. Wait a month or two and the weather will be ideal. Not hot, but not cold. Plus, it's off season so beach house rentals will be really cheap."

"I've never been to the Outer Banks before." Katarina pursed her lips and seemed to consider the prospects. "It might be fun."

"My family used to vacation there every summer. It's great. Some of the towns get a lot of tourist traffic, but there are a few that are secluded."

"But I don't want to be secluded. I want--"

"I know exactly what you want. Someplace out of the way but frequented by enough people to give you a rush. Miles of beautiful sandy beaches, a house with amazing ocean views and huge windows so you can watch the sunrise in the morning and the sunset from your deck at night. Look, leave the details to me. I'll find the perfect place."

I couldn't help but emit a jealous sigh. "I'd love to get out of the city and go to the beach. And the place you're describing sounds perfect."

"Stop it, Stella," Ann said. "Don't say another word about the beach." She rose and went to the window and pressed her forehead against the glass.

I knew what she was seeing. In direct contrast to what I'd envisioned earlier, I was remembering the mounds of dirty snow pushed to the far edge of the sidewalks. Cars driving through slushy streets, people treading carefully lest they slip on a sheet of ice, homeless people asleep on grates. Winter in Baltimore meant runny noses and chilled fingers--despite the overpriced, leather gloves you were wearing. Winter in Baltimore. You had to hate it.

"I wanna go too," Ann whined.

Katarina spun to face her. "But you can't. This would be a romantic weekend for two."

Feeling precisely as Ann, I took up her cause. "It could still be romantic. Look at the pros. If only you and Jim go, you'll only be able to get one of those small beach houses." I held up a hand to stall Katarina. "Those big houses are expensive, even off season, and this wasn't a planned trip. You really want to insist that Jim spend a couple thousand on a beach house this early in your relationship?"

"We could go halfsies."

Ann turned from the window and laughed. "That's it, grind his ego into the dirt. A man would feel emasculated if he couldn't afford to take his lady away for the weekend. He'll be hurt if you offer to pay half. It'll be like you're telling him you don't think he's capable of taking care of you."

"She's right," I started in again, before Katarina could think too hard on our arguments. "If we all go, we can kick in a quarter of the price. We could rent the biggest house on the beach and you'd never have to see any of us."

Katarina considered. "I suppose if Jim and I didn't have to actually see you the entire time it would be okay."

"And when you're ready to have your little adventure, all you do is walk out our front door onto the beach and voila!"

"You think you can find a house like that, Meagan?" Katarina wanted to know.

Meagan eyed me, accusation clearly visible in her eyes. "Yeah. Just give me a few days and I'll see what I can do."

Ann pushed away from the window and cracked her knuckles. "Now, tell us about Steven."

I walked past Katarina and made my way toward the door. "I need a drink for this."

Over Italian margaritas, I told the girls about the catastrophic dinner at my mom's, starting with Sadie the cow and finishing with my mother's invite to Steven for my birthday dinner.

Reclined on the sofa with an oversized margarita glass in her hands, Meagan asked, "So did you tell Jake and Dev?"

"No! Dev is going through his own stuff with his father. I figured it would be selfish of me to start in with my own family problems."

Ann snorted. "Yeah, right. How convenient."
"I'm gonna tell them."
"When?"
"When the time is right."
Ann and Meagan exchanged a look. "Convenient," Ann muttered. "But one thing I can say, I wouldn't miss your birthday dinner for all the tea in China."

* * * *

Journal Entry 3/15/05, 2:22 PM

Boring few days.
Not much happening.
Work is boring.
Can't wait to see Jake and Dev today.

* * * *

2:48 PM

Have I said how bored I am?
Oh, there's the phone. I'm so bored I don't even care if it's my mother.

* * * *

3:51 PM

The day has taken on a dark edge. I'm not seeing Jake or Dev tonight. Seems Dev has a recording session in New York. He's leaving within the hour and he's taking Jake with him. *Argh!* Dev doesn't know how long they'll be gone but he guesses it won't be longer than a day. Already I feel abstinence weighing heavy on me.
I miss them.
Ha! There's the phone again. It must be Dev calling me back to tell me he and Jake are not going and that they cannot bear to be parted from me for another minute.

* * * *

4:02 PM

It was my mother.
The conversation went as follows:
Mother: Stella, has Steven called you?
Me: No
Mother: Are you sure? He said he was going to call you today.

Me: Of course I'm sure. I haven't talked to him since I was at your place.

Mother: Not talked to, dear, spoken with. You haven't spoken with him since you were home.

Argh!

Me: Well I haven't talked to or spoken with him.

Mother: What's wrong honey, you seem irritable today.

Me: Oh, I've got a beep. I should go. It might be Steven.

Mother: *Silence*

Me: Mommy, I have to go. I don't want to miss him.

Mother: All right. Well, tell him I said hello. And try not to say anything too annoying. You don't want to run him off again.

Argh!

Me: I'll do my best not to annoy him. Love you, bye.

So what if I lied about the beep, but what else could I do? I love my mother but sometimes she makes me want to pull my hair out.

* * * *

Journal Entry 3/17/05

I've no idea what time it is other than that it's time for me to have sex. I can't stand this sexual oppression. I fear my feminine part will shrivel in on itself from lack of use.

I miss Jake and Dev.

* * * *

11:00 AM

Spoke with Jake just now.
He has no idea when they're coming home.
Argh!

* * * *

1:27 PM

I was sitting on my living room sofa, clutching a cup of steaming Earl Grey in both hands while David Benoit played on my stereo. I was still coming down from the thirty minute cleaning frenzy, still scanning the room for things I'd missed. I'd dusted the coffee table and armoire, fluffed the fat yellow pillows on my sofa and loveseat, and vacuumed the chic yellow, white, and tan area rug beneath. I'd thrown my drapes open so the amazing view of Mount

Vernon would be visible from the seating area. From where I was, perched on the edge of a cushion, I could see the ornate row houses that spanned my street.

Sighing, I forced my eyes away from the window and to the man sitting opposite me.

Steven pushed a stray micro-braid behind his ear and smiled. Damned if the man wasn't as good-looking as he'd been in high school. Better even. His boyish features had grown into those of a man in his prime. Looking at him had memories of sneaking up the back stairs of my mom's house and into my attic bedroom coming back to me in a rush. I could still remember how perfect the press of his lips were and how wonderfully his body molded to mine.

He'd been my first lover. And for years after that he'd been my only lover. Other than Jake and Dev, I'd only been with two men since.

"You have a beautiful home."

I smiled. "Thank you."

"That's what we do best, Mr. Barry." Ann, dressed in a black pantsuit that was a close match to the forest green one I was wearing, came down the hall with our latest acquisition close on her heels.

"That's why I came," Mr. Barry was saying. "Jack Kennard told me you ladies are the best."

Their voices receded, and I refocused my attention on Steven. "I've always loved Mount Vernon."

"You always said you'd live here one day."

"Yeah, and that I'd have a doctorate and teach at Hopkins."

His milk chocolate eyes slid to the left and right as he looked the room over again. "You don't seem to be suffering too badly. You're a business owner. Isn't that the American dream?"

"I won't lie to you, it is nice. Ann and I have worked very hard to make AIR a success. What about you? What have you been up to? My mom says you're a financial analyst now. What happened to music?"

He uncrossed his legs, reached for the mug of tea on his side of the coffee table, then seemed to think better of it. With an audible sigh, he began to rub his temples. "What have I been up to ... that's sort of what I was hoping to talk with you about today." Steven settled back, sinking into the downy fluff, his eyes fixed unwaveringly on mine. He sucked in a breath then exhaled. His broad shoulders seemed on the verge of ripping the thin white shirt he had on.

Uh-oh. Whatever he had to say, it wouldn't be good.

"You know I think you're wonderful, right?"

"Yeah, sure."

"And you know I wouldn't trade any of what we shared for the world."

"Yeah, so."

"So--" he paused, gazed at my ceiling, "--so I didn't want to say anything to your mom, but, I'm not really looking to rehash the past."

Did he just say what I think he said? "Who said anything about rehashing the past?"

"Come on, Stella, it's me, Steven. You don't have to pretend with me."

"I repeat, who said anything about rehashing the past? We had dinner at my mom's house. I don't see how that's rehashing the past."

"Your mom told me how lonely you've been."

I rocketed to my feet. "She what?"

He stood, his hands held up before him. "Calm down, Stella. Don't get mad. She loves you; she just wants you to be happy. Unfortunately, it can't be with me."

"What?"

"Look, Stella, it's not that I think there's anything wrong with you."

"Wrong with me? Of course there's nothing wrong with me, don't be an ass."

"God knows you're the best lover I ever had."

I was too stunned to respond to that statement.

"It's just that … well--"

"Well what?"

He let his arms drop and exhaled again. "I'm making a mess of this, aren't I? I didn't want things to go this way."

"Well what?" I demanded again, this time through clenched teeth.

"It's not you, it's me."

"No shit."

"It's just that I'm at an age where I'm ready to settle down, start a family."

"And I'm not?"

"I'm sure you are. I'm not saying you're not. You mom says you've been looking for a man for years. Only thing is, I just don't think I could fall in love with you, Stella."

My mouth fell open and hung there, suspended in mid-air.

"At least not in the way you deserve to be loved."

"Who the hell ever said I wanted you to love me?"

He shrugged. "Your mom."

I counted to ten. When that didn't work, I counted to thirty. When I began to feel I could continue this conversation without going completely over the edge, I informed him that, "For your information, I'm not looking for a man. I'm already involved with one." I was on the verge of saying I was involved with two, but didn't want to seem too overzealous to prove my point.

My bastard high school boyfriend had the nerve to smirk. "Is that right?"

"That's right."

"So why did your mom beg me to come to dinner on Saturday?"

I snorted. "Who the hell knows?"

"You don't have to get defensive, Stella. I'm just trying to be honest with you. I think you deserve that after all we've been through."

To hear him talk you'd think being in a relationship with me was like braving Desert Storm.

"Honest, eh. Well, why don't I give a go at this honesty thing, then." I closed the distance between us and shoved my finger into his chest. "I honestly want you to get out of my house. How's that for honest?"

"Stella, don't be like that. Did I say how amazing the sex was?"

"Get out!"

He didn't waste any time making his way to my front door. I was close on his heels, was even nice enough to open the door for him and wait while he slipped into his coat.

He turned to face me, that annoying smirk frozen to his face.

"Don't you dare feel sorry for me. I don't require sympathy, especially not from you."

"It was nice seeing you again."

I grunted.

"I'll see you on your birthday."

"The hell you will."

"Your mom invited me. I don't want to disappoint her. Besides, I'm looking forward to meeting this so-called man of yours." With that, he walked out of my house, to the stairs, and trotted out of sight.

* * * *

7:21 PM

I'm not unlovable, am I? How could Steven think he couldn't fall in love with me? I'd been with him longer than I'd been with any man and had shown him more of myself than I'd ever shown any other boyfriend. How could he say he didn't think he could love me?

How much do you want to bet that Jake and Dev are off in New York right now trying to figure out ways to dump me? I bet they're telling each other that their little excursion into heterosexual/ménage sex was fun while it lasted, but is at an end.

I'm not unlovable, am I?

* * * *

7:29 PM

Maybe I should call Jake and Dev and demand they tell me the truth. Maybe I should call them and call the whole thing off.

Maybe I should call Ann.

Yes, I think that's what I'll do. I'll call Ann.

* * * *

7:32 PM

Crap! I forgot. Ann is out with Gerard tonight. It's why she didn't have time to do anything but race out of the apartment after Mr. Barry left. I didn't even have time to tell her what that horror of an ex-boyfriend said to me.

Perhaps that's a good thing. Perhaps I should be alone and think.

What I should do is call my mother and tell her off.

Maybe I'll rent a movie.

I really don't think I'm unlovable.

Chapter Six

Journal Entry 3/21/05, 11:51 AM

"Which do you think looks better? The red, the black, or the purple?"

Popping the last bit of hot pretzel into my mouth, I gave the garments draped over Meagan's arm a once over. Dressed in her gray and red wool suit with her honey hair pulled up into a French twist, she looked wholly disreputable holding the lacey G-strings.

"Take all three," I suggested.

Beside me, Katarina snorted. "You can't buy the same panties in different colors, Stella."

"Why the hell not?" Ann wanted to know.

"Because you just can't. It's tacky."

"Says who?"

Katarina stared at Ann for a moment, seemed to take in Ann's frayed Levis, her three year old DKNY shirt, her vintage leather jacket and her worn winter boots. Katarina gave her head a sad shake. Blonde waves tumbled over her suede-sheathed shoulders and bounced across her designer blouse. "Says everyone."

Ann rolled her eyes. "That's the stupidest thing I've ever heard, Katarina. Who the hell cares if I buy three of the same panties? Gerard sure as shit could care less." Ann looked at me and winked. "It's what's in the panties that Gerard--"

"Stop!" Katarina interrupted. "I don't want to hear any more. You're so vulgar."

"Another thing my betrothed loves about me."

"Have you told the parents yet?" I asked.

"Not until we set a date. Hey Katarina, wanna know what else Gerard likes to see me in ... ?"

Deciding my best bet was to ignore both of them, I went to Meagan, who'd been moving through the panty section as though she were on a mission. "Red's always good," I said.

She eyed the panties in her hand. "You don't think red's too obvious?"

"I thought obvious was what you wanted."

Meagan began to nod, the nod turned into a shake and a sigh, then she shrugged. "Shit Stella. What's going on with me? I'm never this indecisive. And about friggin' underpants of all things. I hate this."

Two hours ago, Meagan had made an emergency conference call to Ann, Katarina and me. She told us she'd had an epiphany that had scared the hell out of her. Apparently, sometime in the last few weeks, her on again, off again relationship with Peter (The sexy Taye Diggs look alike she introduced me to last month at Club Blue) had gone on again. And with a vengeance.

"I think I'm falling in love with him," she'd confided in a whisper over the telephone.

None of us knew what to say. Meagan was a confirmed bachelorette, after all. She was the original playa'. Nobody had seen this coming. Meagan falling in love was big. I hadn't been this surprised since I heard Charlie Sheen was settling down with Denise Richardson. But damn, they just broke up so I guess that's not the best example.

"Meet me at eleven at Vicky's in the Gallery," Meagan told us.

"On Pratt Street?" Katarina wanted to know.

True, there was only one Gallery, but it was a perfectly legitimate question. Pratt Street was Inner Harbor territory, which was to say, domain of the tourists. Locals didn't frequent the malls of the Inner Harbor. Everything at the Gallery was over merchandised and overpriced.

"I'm telling him tonight," Meagan explained. "I need something to wear. There's no time to go anywhere else."

So there we were, taking our lunch break at Victoria's Secret.

"At least Peter's not likely to tell you you're unlovable."

Meagan looked up from the rack of clothes and met my gaze. "Which one of those bastards said you were--"

"No, it wasn't Jake or Dev." I sidled closer, looked over my shoulder to make sure Katarina was far enough away so she wouldn't overhear. She was half way across the store, trying unsuccessfully to escape Ann. "Steven came over yesterday."

"What? And he told you that you're unlovable?"

"In a nutshell." I looked for Katarina again and saw she was making her way toward us, Ann hot on her heels. "Basically my mom filled his head with some garbage about me pining away for him all these years. Not only have I been missing Steven, according to my mother, but I've been completely unable to get any man to give me a second look. She made me sound like Quasimodo."

"And that idiot believed her?"

"Worse. He came to my house with the express purpose of letting me down easy. He said I was good in the sack, but not wife material." Relaying the events of the previous day to Meagan was like reliving the humiliation all over again. "I'm wife material, right?"

Meagan whapped me on the shoulder with a pair of hot pink panties. "Don't be stupid, Stella. You're not going to let a guy you dated in high school give you a complex, are you? You and I both know that some day you're going to make some man ... or men ... a great wife. So what if Steven doesn't think he could fall in love with you. Maybe he couldn't. That's not a reflection on you. Maybe you couldn't fall in love with him again, either. And that's not a reflection on him. As to your mom, well, I love the woman but you know how she is."

Judgmental and interfering. "So you don't think the only reason Jake and Dev are hanging with me is because ..." I was going to say, because all of the freaky things I let them do to me, but thought better of it, "... of sex?"

"I don't know Jake or Dev well enough to say what their intentions with you are, but I know you. You're beautiful, funny, and intelligent--any man would be lucky to have you. The fact that you're good in bed is a bonus. Any man with half a brain would see that."

"What's even more annoying is the fact that Steven's planning on coming to the birthday dinner my mom is having for me."

"Why?"

"Because he says he was invited and doesn't want to disappoint my mother. What I think is that the only reason he's coming now is to see if I really have a boyfriend or not."

She shrugged. "So bring Jake and Dev."

"What! My mother would kill me. I can't bring them."

Strolling to another rack, she shook her head. "I don't know what to tell you. If I were you I'd bring them, or at least one of them, but I'm not you."

Before I could respond, I was engulfed in a fragrant cloud of watermelon scented body splash.

"I think Peter's a great guy," Katarina--the source of the sweet aroma--pushed between Meagan and me. "I was hoping he'd be the one."

"I still can't believe it," Ann said. "Are you sure, Meagan?"

Meagan had discarded the pink panties and took up a very sheer, very see through black negligee. She winked at me and smiled at Ann. "I am."

"You guys know what this means?" Katarina asked, but didn't bother waiting for a response. "It means for the first time ever we're all in relationships at the same time."

I decided it would be more advantageous for me to keep my mouth shut. I love Meagan and Katarina dearly, and wouldn't trade them for all the jewels in the world, but they had originally greeted the news of my relationship with Jake and Dev like a couple of frigid old ladies. They doubted the legitimacy of such a joining, expressed suspicion concerning Jake and Dev's motivations, and had actually questioned my sanity. Though they'd eventually come around, I wasn't entirely convinced they thought what I was doing was a good idea.

"We should all go out and celebrate," Katarina announced.

"Let's see how tonight goes first," Meagan said. "I'm not even sure if Peter wants to get serious."

"If he does," Katarina continued doggedly, "we should do something together. Who knows when this will happen again."

Ann pushed a stray lock of hair out of her eyes and crossed to a rack of overpriced gowns. "They're men, Katarina. It's not that big a deal. And Meagan, you and I both know Peter is not going to turn you down. Men aren't capable of turning you down. Hey, check out this nightgown. Is that silk?"

"I'd say The Oak Room, but we always go there." Katarina fingered the slinky black slip of the garment Ann was salivating over and nodded her approval. "One hundred percent silk. Must feel like heaven on the skin."

"How much is it?"

Katarina eyed the price tag and grimaced. "A hundred and nine. But worth every penny, I bet."

"How about Club Blue?" Meagan suggested, grinning at me.

Ann had told them about my faux kidnapping. Though Katarina didn't think there was anything funny about Dev donning a leather mask and carrying me out of a fetish club, Meagan had thought it amusing in a sexually debauched sort of way. I didn't go into details about what had happened once I was at Jake's, despite their pleading and begging for me to paint them a vivid picture of what sex with two men was like.

"We can have dinner at Jake and Dev's," I offered. "Dev's an amazing cook."

Ann seemed to forget the gown she'd been eyeing; Katarina whirled around, lips parted in a smile; and Meagan raised one perfectly arched brow.

"We finally get to see the secret lair?" Meagan was the first to say.

"Jake won't mind?" Katarina asked a moment later.

"I think Jake would like having you over. He's not an ogre you know."

"He has a condo at Harbor Towers, right?" Katarina went on. "I've been dying to see the inside of that place for years. I bet his place is great."

Jake and Dev had the nicest home I'd ever been in. Still, I shrugged casually and waved the comment off. "It's nice enough."

"Bullshit!" Ann grabbed the gown off the rack and started for the register. "That's not what you told me. You said their place was amazing. You said ..."

I didn't hear the rest because my cell phone started ringing.

"Yeah?" I said into the transmitter.

"Kitten, are you busy?"

"Dev!" Warmth suffused my body at the sound of his buttery smooth voice. I had to pause on my way to the register so I could lean against a shelf full of pantyhose packages and catch my breath. "I'm shopping with the girls."

"Really. Where?"

"Vicky's ... Victoria's Secret."

"You gonna buy something nice to wear for Jake and me?"

"I'm here to help Meagan shop. Oh, she's on her way to the register."

"Too bad. Are you at the Victoria's Secret in the Gallery?"

I nodded then realized he couldn't see me. "Yeah."

"Good. Meet me out front in five minutes. I'm in the Jag."

"But--" It was no good. He'd already hung up.

When had Dev come home? Dear God, maybe he wanted to have sex.

A girl could hope.

"What's up?" Ann asked and came toward me with Vicky's bag tucked protectively under one arm.

"You guys finished already?" I asked.

"Yep. Meagan got a fancy red nightie. Who was on the phone?"

I followed Ann into the mall and toward the escalator before answering. Dev, gorgeous creature that he was, always had a mind-numbing affect on me. I still hadn't adjusted to the fact that I was in a relationship with him *and* Jake. Everything felt so new. I got chills when I heard either man's voice, broke out in a sweat whenever I saw them, became ravenous with sexual need anytime they were near. I figured I'd done something extraordinary in a past life to deserve such treats as Jake and Dev.

The sound of Dev's voice was enough to rouse a kind of erotic desperation in me that I'd never experienced in my pre-Jake/Dev days. Knowing I'd have the unforeseen delight of seeing him in a few minutes, of being able to touch him, had anticipation humming through me. I needed a few moments to collect myself before I even considered speaking.

When I was stepping onto the down escalator and felt more in control, I confided, "Dev's home and he's coming." After the adolescent catcalls and hoots, I continued. "We don't have any client meetings scheduled for the rest of the day, do we Ann?"

"Just one, but I can handle her," Ann said, grinning. "I'll handle any inquiries too. Other than that, all I have left to do today is to put the finishing touches on the White and Beecham presentation. Will you be back before I go home?"

I didn't have a clue. In all honesty, I didn't know if I was even going anywhere with Dev. He could very well be showing up to tell me something, nothing more. Yet, there I was, heart slamming into my chest, blood pressure rising, and hormones on full alert as if I'd just planned some secret rendezvous.

Damn! This wasn't good. I was getting way too attached to Dev and Jake for my own good. Things had definitely progressed too far if I was willing to forget everything else at the drop of a hat as soon as Dev said so.

"You shouldn't be so accessible," Katarina said, as though she could read my mind.

We made our way across the ground floor of the mall and toward the outer doors.

"I'm not being overly accessible," I lied. "He sounded concerned about something on the phone so I'm going to go with him and see what's up. That's all. I don't think that makes me too accessible. Hell, if you called me and needed help I'd drop everything for you too. Not that I'm dropping everything." I groaned.

Katarina eyed Meagan. It was a look that said, "See, told you."

Meagan nodded sagely and pushed through the doors. "Maybe you should play hard to get with these guys every now and again, make them work for it."

"I do make them work for it," I said, shoving past them and dodging the people traipsing up and down the sidewalk so I could commence my search. I went to the edge of Calvert Street and scanned the lunchtime traffic for Dev. I stared up at the tall buildings around me, as though Dev might be hiding out within one, but came up short.

"That's it Stella," Ann mocked. "Play it close to the cuff."

I whirled around, prepared to make a cutting remark, when I saw the Jag whip into the taxi stand on Pratt Street in front of The Gallery, annoying a whole host of cabbies. A moment later, Dev leaned on the horn.

Forgetting my indignation with Ann, along with my pride, self-respect, and self-control, I half skipped, half jogged to the car. I was glad I'd worn jeans and sneakers instead of the skirt and pumps I'd had on earlier today. I wouldn't have made it to him half as fast had I been waylaid by heels.

The door of the Jag flew wide as Dev shoved it open with his foot. He appeared in the opening with a red Oriole's cap pulled low on his forehead and a self-satisfied smirk on his lips. His hair was tucked ruthlessly under the rim of the cap, a habit he had whenever he went out and didn't want to be recognized as Cinder.

The black jeans fit him perfectly, snug enough for me to enjoy the sight of every bulge and protrusion as I neared. He had his leather jacket fastened though, so I couldn't see what shirt he was wearing, or even if he was wearing one. March or not, too often Dev went out sans shirt, with only a leather coat to cover him. It was a practice I was willing to wager he'd learned from Jake.

I paused, just out of reach, and stared into his eyes. Though it may sound crazy, I love this stage of a relationship when everything is fresh. I still got butterflies whenever I was around Dev and Jake, and I still felt awkward as a schoolgirl getting her first kiss. The desire to touch Dev, to run my hands over him, was nearly too strong to control, but I managed.

My lips twitched as I tried to give him my best, come-hither smile. I guessed the coy act would have been more convincing had I not run like a wild woman to greet him.

"That just won't do, kitten," he said, stretching forward to grasp me. "I've been thinking about you since I left."

I allowed myself to be captured and drawn forward. As his arms encircled my waist I slithered against him, reveling in his body heat. It was indescribably decadent to be this close to Dev, to have his hands on me and know his desire to be alone was as strong as my own. More than anything he could have said to convince me such was the case, the expanding in the crotch of his pants was all the convincing I needed.

A cool jet of air hissed between my teeth as my sex tightened. Anticipatory tingles shimmied up and down my spine. One look at Dev, just a few minutes in his presence was enough to make me horny as a cat in heat.

He guided my arms around his waist and lowered his face to mine. When our lips touched I wanted to press closer and lose myself in him. I needed to feel every inch, to know the weight of his body on mine. I thought about easing into the back of the car and pulling him in behind me. I'd lie across the seat and guide him in until he was lying across me, pinning me to the supple leather.

When Dev's tongue glided along my lower lip, coherent thought fled. Pure female need surged to the surface of my consciousness. Standing on tiptoe, I squeezed his backside and opened my mouth to him, let him slip inside and deepen the kiss.

"Hello!"

I wanted to scream in protest when Dev stood back and put distance between us again. "Ladies," he said, by way of greeting my friends.

Glad to be acknowledged, Katarina uncrossed her arms. "Where are you taking Stella?"

If she'd been talking to Jake, his response would have been, "None of your business." But since it was Dev, and because Dev had more decorum than Jake, Katarina got a more palatable response. "Shopping," he said. "Do you need a ride somewhere?"

Despite the fact that Katarina's office was on Pratt Street, she seemed to consider the offer.

"No," I said, before she could take him up on it. "Katarina works here on Pratt Street and Meagan's office is around the corner on St. Paul. And Ann has her truck. She'll give them a ride if they need one." I gave the girls a brief wave. "See you guys later. Call me in the morning Meagan. Let me know how it goes."

As I made my way to the passenger side of the car, I tried to tell myself I was rushing because the cabbies seemed on the verge of jumping Dev. It wasn't as if I was ditching my friends. In another minute everyone would be heading back to work anyway.

I slid into the car and realized I was alone. Dev was standing in his open doorway, mired in one-sided conversations with Katarina and Meagan, though I'm not sure conversation was the appropriate word. Interrogation seemed more fitting.

I leaned across the driver's seat and gave his jeans a tug.

"How old are you?" I could hear Katarina demanding. "Stella won't tell us how old you are and I'd like to know."

"If you're in love with Jake ..." Meagan was saying at the same time, "you are in love with him, right? Then what do you want with Stella?"

Damn. This was the first occasion they'd had to question Dev. I could see they were perfectly willing to take full advantage of the opportunity.

I gave Dev another tug. Once he answered one question he was doomed. They'd close in on him.

"Is this just a sex thing?" Katarina was saying. "If it is, I think that sucks."

When he began sputtering, I climbed over the driver's seat and leaned out far enough to eye Katarina and Meagan. "We're leaving now." Saying this, I backed into the car and pulled Dev with me.

Dev got in, gave me a self-deprecating grin and pulled into traffic.

* * * *

1:27 PM

How in the hell did I end up at not one, but two shopping malls today? That's all I want to know. Not that I'm complaining, mind you. I'm never opposed to having a man take me out to buy a new dress, but I was more than a little put out that instead of heading to his place for fun, Dev took me to the 'burbs. Not only that, he'd managed to find Arundel Mills, the most obnoxiously large mall within a fifty-mile radius of Baltimore. The place was a shopping monstrosity. And I don't say that lightly. For instance, we entered the mall near the movie theatre, though the words "movie theatre" are in no way an accurate description of the actual structure. That the architects had grandiose visions when drawing up the building plans was obvious. The Egyptian themed, "Muvico" had soaring columns, hieroglyphs painted artfully along the entrance corridor, and statues of Egyptian gods positioned at various points along the entrance, each leering disapprovingly at passing shoppers. It was nice, but a little overwhelming.

Once we were in the mall, we stood poised at the mall entrance for approximately five minutes, staring dumbly around and trying to figure out which direction we should go. Despite the fact that it was a weekday, the mall was crowded. There were hordes of people heading in every direction. Some were on their way to a movie, others made a beeline for the music store, but the majority was traipsing up and down the halls in no apparent rush to go anywhere.

Seeing the mass of bodies moving about, I couldn't help but wonder, didn't people have jobs anymore? And what about school? The place was jam-packed.

Dev clasped my hand and gave me a tug that had me taking a step toward him. "I'm wearing a black pinstripe tuxedo for the ball," he said. "Do you have a favorite color?"

Quick as a flash, I forgot about the people trudging through the mall around us. I found myself staring at his delectable lips, wishing he would kiss me. Save the all-to-brief taste he'd given me outside the Gallery, Dev hadn't made any attempt to treat me to his lips again. It was frustrating.

"Focus kitten. Think party dress."

"But I missed you and you haven't even told me how your sessions went. Can't we spend some time alone before we shop? And where the hell is Jake?"

"Sessions went great and Jake had to work. He said to tell you he's looking forward to the ball. Now let's focus on finding a dress. I was thinking we'd find one at Hot Topic but I've no idea where the store is. Do you know?"

Dress hell. Slipping my free hand around his waist and standing on my toes, I tried to force him to kiss me. I let my breasts press into his chest, melded my body to his. His warmth seeped into me, drawing a soft moan from the back of my throat.

Despite the stirring I felt between his legs, Dev, damn the man, tilted his head away and raised a brow. "You have a one-track mind, don't you? No sex, Stella. Not until we find a dress for the ball. I feel quite a bit like your fairy godmother right now."

I remained on my toes a moment longer, hoping he'd relent. "One itsy, bitsy little kiss?" I batted my lashes and gave him a pout. When he laughed, I didn't take it as a good sign. With a few choice words, I settled flat on my feet. "Since when did you become so sanctimonious?"

"I'm not. But I refuse to be distracted from the goal. Dress first, after that ..." He gave me a heavy-lidded stare and dragged his tongue over his bottom lip. The exquisite slowness of the move brought visions of hot sex to my mind.

"You're cruel, Dev. Jake never teases me."

"I'm not Jake. When I fuck you, I want you desperate for it."

Dev eased from my grasp and started forward, leading me away from Muvico and deeper into the mall. "So, do you have a favorite color?" He asked again a few minutes later.

"Didn't you even miss me a little bit?"

"Jake and I missed you terribly. Sex wasn't the same without you. I wasn't home an hour before I came to get you. Now let's focus on finding a dress."

It was obvious Dev wouldn't be persuaded into sharing an erotic interlude with me, so I tried to do as he suggested and focus on buying a dress. "You don't have to buy me a dress, you know. I have plenty to choose from at home."

He took hold of my hand and held me so his hot palm was flush against mine. When he squeezed me a fresh wave of arousal vibrated through me. "Maybe I want to buy you a dress."

I was so pleased by this statement that I nearly emitted a girlish giggle. I managed to suppress it. "Okay. I'll cooperate."

We stopped in a store I figured had purchased stock in Baltimore Gas and Electric. Bright, florescent light shone from the ceiling, thoroughly illuminating the pastel wears on display throughout the shop. Skimpy summer dresses in various hues of pink, orange, teal, and green hung on racks. The dresses were so tiny I had to wonder exactly who could put these clothes on and hope to cover any of their more private parts. The garments were nearly microscopic. Also short on material were the short-shorts, micro-mini's, and halter-tops. Didn't people wear clothes that covered them anymore?

When I felt a hand shove my coat aside then a finger dip into the waistband at the back of my pants, drawing me back a step, I was pulled from my thoughts.

"Stella," Dev said, sliding another finger into my waistband. "You have any shorts like these?" He held an object up for my inspection.

I scanned the garment in question: a pair of very pink, very minuscule, short-shorts. As a rule, I didn't wear anything that would show that much of my butt unless I was on the beach. "No."

Another finger squiggled over my waistband. "I think they'd look great on you."

I looked at Dev, saw searing lust in his eyes, then took the shorts. "But I have wanted to get a pair."

So what! I'm not the first woman to tell a white lie for a man, and I won't be the last. I'm also not the first woman to contemplate wearing some ridiculous item of clothing to make a man happy.

As I walked to the changing rooms at the back of the store, a tiny voice in my head tried to convince me the shorts were too "young" for me, but I ignored it. I could pull off micro clothing as well as any twenty-something. However, poised in the fitting room with said shorts on a bit later, I was beginning to have my doubts. Short, didn't really begin to describe what I was wearing. I stared at my reflection and wondered if they were supposed to look like that.

A copious amount of flesh lay bared for all to see and I doubted, even with the promise of sex hovering in the air, I could wear something so skimpy in public.

"Do you have them on yet?" Dev called. From the nearness of his voice, I knew he was poised just beyond the curtain. "Try this top on with them."

A bikini type shirt appeared over the curtain rod, Dev's bejeweled fingers clasping the item as if it were gold. For a moment I merely contemplated the object, wondered how far I was willing to go to get some action.

Maybe a little further, I mused, and then grabbed the shirt.

Once I had it on and saw my reflection, I couldn't help but laugh. *If the girls could see me now.* Hell, they'd probably have me committed. My breasts didn't so much rest in the narrow sliver of cups the top offered, as much as they warred against it. One quick move, one wrong turn and my wears would be on display for all to see.

I was willing to do a lot to make Dev happy, but this was where I drew the line.

"Are you dressed?" Dev called.

"I don't think these are gonna work, Dev." *I know these aren't gonna work.*

"Let me see."

Shaking my head at my own bemused reflection, I said, "I don't think so."

A moment later, the curtain was shoved aside. Before it could settle back into its closed position, Dev was standing beside me, a faraway look on his face.

Hands on hips, I turned to face him. "Dev," I whispered in my most stern voice. "You can't be in here."

"Turn around." His voice was low and rich with sexual innuendo.

I turned.

I displayed the posterior view for him and he let out a strangled groan. "We're buying these."

"What about the dress?"

"We'll get you a dress too, and maybe a few mini-skirts."

That wasn't what I wanted to hear. I didn't want to own these clothes. I'd never wear them. I spun to face him. "Dev, I can't go in public like this. I'd be arrested."

He stepped close and fitted his palms to my very exposed bottom. "Who said anything about going out in public? This is for home. For Jake and me." He squeezed and drew me forward until my body fit snuggly to his. "Baby, you have no idea how sexy you look right now."

I squirmed free of him and stepped back.

Dev advanced.

Chapter Seven

Before I realized what was happening, he was on me. I released a surprised yelp when the cold glass of the mirror met my skin. The discomfort, however, was quickly forgotten.

His arms quivered when he set them against the wall on either side of me, as though to actually touch me would be too much for him. He moved in with the speed of a panther and gave me a sexy growl as he closed the distance between us.

Then his lips were on me, and all conscious thought evaporated.

Gentle as a dove, his lips moved over mine. Despite the ravenous desire I saw in his eyes, the touch was hesitant. Our lips brushed, the wet creases of his mouth inciting a fire in me. Eager for this intimacy, desperate for it, I opened to him. Of their own accord my arms reached for him, pulled him close. I stood on my toes, so desperate for more than a chaste kiss I marveled that I could stand on my own two feet.

"I want you so bad right now," he muttered, then dove deeper.

He tasted like paradise. His lips, his breath, his skin. There wasn't any part of him I didn't delight in feasting on. I lost myself in him, reveled in the feel of his tongue plunging into my mouth and feeding. His fingers grazed my scalp as he tangled his hands in my hair and pulled my head back, positioning me so he could delve deeper.

Our tongues danced; I was in a frenzy for more.

Then he released me and stepped away.

"Not a good place," he said, chest heaving.

I couldn't disagree, though I had to force myself not to twist a finger in a belt loop and drag him forward again. Instead, I nodded.

He stared at me with hooded eyes, an evil grin spreading on his lips. "We're gonna finish this later, kitten."

Saying this, he slipped out of the dressing stall and left me alone, trying to catch my breath.

* * * *

5:21 PM

Four hundred dollars later, I teetered around on three-inch heels while Dev struggled under the weight of our shopping bags.

It took us an hour and a half to traverse the first half of the mall ... and I'm not exaggerating. My feet hurt, my ears had tired of the incessant chatter going on around me, and I was horny. I'd lost the thrill of shopping a few stores back. When I left the girls at the Gallery I was primed to do something sexy with Dev. Earlier, Dev had led me to believe he too wanted to enjoy a few carnal delights, but so far, that hadn't happened.

I'd lost count as to exactly how many stores we'd been in, but it seemed we'd purchased something from every one of them. More shorts, micro-mini's, halter-tops, shoes, a few pairs of jeans--something I would actually wear in public--and more dresses than I figured I'd ever wear. Including the dress I currently had on. An incredibly short, pink and green, floral print baby doll dress. We'd found the heels in a Nine West outlet. They weren't the kind I typically purchased for myself. I wasn't big on pink. Frankly, I was a little surprised to learn just how fond Dev was of the color. In any case, the shoes were fashioned to look like ... well ... slutty Mary Jane's. Basically, I looked like an overgrown schoolgirl with very bad intentions.

For about the two hundred thousandth time since I'd allowed Dev to convince me into donning the ridiculous outfit, I thanked God for the long winter coat I was wearing. Presently, it was buttoned from my ankles to my chin.

"Stick a fork in me, I'm done." I cuddled closer to Dev, eased an arm around his waist and squeezed. "Dev. Let's pick up Jake and go to my place."

One look at me, and Dev knew exactly what I wanted. He was silent for a few beats, his lush lips open and poised for speech. "What a bad little girl."

"You promised that we'd--"

He shushed me. "Jake is working late. He's catching up from being gone for so long."

"Then lets you and I go to my place."

"Are you hungry? There's the food court." He pointed to the semicircle of tables and brightly lit fast food restaurants to the left of us. "We can grab something to hold us till we get home."

I thought Dev was being more than a little unreasonable. "I'm not hungry, Dev, I'm horny. Sorry, but my hormones don't move on your friggin' time schedule."

Dev stopped and gazed at me. "Is that right?" With a shrug, he turned and started for the food court. I supposed I was meant to follow.

So what if I did.

Bloody hell, I wasn't hungry. Did the man have a hearing problem or was he stupid? Would I have to do something drastic or ... ? I never finished that thought. At that moment I saw he wasn't taking me to the food court but to the hall at the back of the food court that led to the restrooms. We entered a sterile corridor, the sound of my heels clipping the floor echoed around us. He led me down the first hallway and to the right down a second hall where we were far out of sight of mall traffic. He came to an abrupt halt, backed me into a wall, and studied me. "Unfortunately for you, Stella," Dev began, casually removing his hat and dropping it in a bag, "you're not in control. I am." His stance was more telling of just how much control he had over the situation. Standing so close I had to crane my head back just to see his face, Dev loomed over me. Even with the numerous shopping bags he was holding, Dev seemed one hundred percent male. And my body reacted to this fact immediately.

My sex gave a hungry clench even as I blinked. I looked away, thinking maybe if I got my eyes off him I could regain my mental footing.

"Look at me, Stella."

Slowly, I tilted my head toward him again and raised my eyes to his. Lips set in a determined frown and his wavy brown hair sexily mussed, he looked feral.

"Good girl. If I do anything you don't like, tell me to stop. Understand?"

The question, posed with such seriousness, was a clear indication to me that we were playing a sex game now. A carnal game of domination and submission of the sort that I'd come to love these last few months. "Yes, I understand."

"I want you to open your coat for me."

Shit! I should have learned by now that it was never a good idea to call Dev's bluff. Eccentric that he was, Dev was always ready to rise to whatever challenge came his way, and he had taken me demanding that I was ready for action *now* as a definite challenge.

"What are you waiting for, kitten? I told you to open your coat."

I glanced to the left and right to see if anyone was coming along the corridor. It remained empty, but I didn't know how long that would last. "What if someone comes?"

Dev settled the shopping bags on the floor, eyes on me the entire time. Speaking in a slow, measured voice, he said again. "Open your coat, Stella."

I began to glance up and down the corridor once more, but was stopped cold when Dev demanded. "Eyes on me. My opinion is the only one you need to care about right now."

Feeling a little stunned by Dev's sudden transformation from shopping buddy to Dom, I lifted shaky hands and set about releasing the buttons on my coat, as ordered. When I was finished, I met Dev's stare.

Unlike Jake, who could remain stony eyed until his climax, Dev didn't mind expressing his emotions. However, with his deep brown eyes narrowed to thin slits and his lips pursed, I wasn't sure what he was thinking.

"Hold it open," he said.

The desire to see if anyone was coming was nearly too strong for me to overcome. Nevertheless, I clasped the flaps of my coat and spread them wide. Hot air whooshed past my bare legs and I shivered. In my skimpy clothing I nearly felt naked without my coat to cover me. But I didn't move.

"Good girl," Dev breathed. He reached between his legs and gave his crotch a squeeze. "Now, baby, I want you to take your panties off and give them to me."

I swallowed. Hard. "But Dev--"

"Do it, Stella."

With lust making smooth movement impossible, I bent and slid my fingers under the short skirt of my dress until I found the waistband of my panties. I drew them down my thighs, over my knees until they pooled on the floor at my feet. The need to have Dev inside me grew. I didn't know why such displays of domination aroused me, couldn't fathom how this had happened to me. All I knew was if he wasn't buried inside me soon, I'd explode from pent up sexual yearning.

Bending low, I clasped the panties then stood and set them in Dev's waiting hand.

He stuffed them in his coat pocket. "Good girl." Dev moved closer, forced his body so firmly to mine that I nearly swooned with joy.

Our lips met in a slow, erotic kiss. Then he surprised me by sliding a finger along my wet nether lips. He prodded me open, and slid his finger inside. "We're gonna play a little game, kitten."

His finger glided along the moist walls of my pussy, found my G-spot and tickled. Whimpering at this delicious contact, I wondered how long I'd be able to stay on my feet.

"You wanna play a game with me?" he slipped a second finger within.

Heat descended on me and need flowed through my body like buttery smooth chocolate. My legs trembled. The delicious thrill of Dev's touch was nearly too much. Too much and not nearly enough. To my starved body, his fingers were magic, but I wanted more than fingers. "Yeah."

He captured my lips again, nudged them open with a flick of his tongue and probed within.

I thought I'd melt into a quivering mass of Jell-o on the floor at his feet. The touch of his tongue, the feel of his fingers as he penetrated deep, withdrew, then sank inside again was a wonderful torture. The fact that we were in public should have given me pause, but it didn't.

Dev drew back and glanced at his watch. "For the rest of the night, Stella, I own you." He let his eyes rove my body. "I figure, why let that adorable baby doll dress and those shoes go to waste."

"But what about Jake?"

Speaking against my spread lips he said, "Until I say otherwise, kitten, that sweet little pussy belongs to me and me alone." He found my clit with a finger and began a slow tease. He moved his fingers in languorous strokes that had an inferno blazing inside of me.

"Dev," I begged against his mouth. Suddenly so desperate for him I'd forgotten where we were. "Please."

Dev released my lips and grinned wickedly. His finger continued to dance over my nub, drawing me inexorably to climax. "I love how pliant you are when you're turned on. So very docile."

I hated that word, and Dev knew it. No doubt, that was precisely why he used it. But I was too far gone to quibble over words. I wanted Dev, was frantic for Dev, so docile it was.

He stepped back, a movement that put an immediate end to the delicious tickling between my legs.

Eyes on me, he lifted his fingers, still glistening from my juices, and raised them to his mouth. He sucked the fingers clean. "You taste good, kitten."

I opened my mouth, but remained still and silent, waiting for his next direction.

"Button your coat, Stella, then follow me."

I wanted to protest, wanted to beg him to finish what he'd started, but thought better of it. No matter how horny I was, we couldn't very well get busy in the hall to the restrooms. Sooner or later we'd be caught. That nobody had wandered down the hall thus far was something of a minor miracle.

With the promise of sex, I hurried to clasp my buttons.

Chapter Eight

6:24 PM

We sat side by side in the car, me trembling with repressed desire. I wanted Dev's hands on me again so bad I could scarce breathe.

"Relax, Stella." Dev said as he drove north on I-95. "This'll be fun."

He glanced at me. A curl fell over an eye, making him seem boyishly innocent for a moment. Then he turned away to face the road again and the moment was gone.

* * * *

7:07 PM

I turned on the lights in my foyer, and out of habit, nearly walked back to the office to check for messages. The place was dark, so I figured Ann had left for the day. Still, I thought it prudent to double check. "Ann!" I called, hoping I wouldn't get an answer.

I didn't.

Running AIR out of my house was damned convenient, but at times like this, when I wanted the place to myself, I second guessed the wisdom of it. But tonight, Ann was gone for the day.

Heaving a sigh of relief, I turned to Dev who'd already removed his coat and was holding it out to me. His face was flushed pink from the cold, but not even a blush on the cheeks was enough to disguise the lascivious intent etched on his face. His lips twitched as he watched me, his eyes narrowed as if he were thinking of numerous ways he could entertain himself with my body.

I'd never been alone with Dev like this before. Always, whenever sex was a possibility it was either Jake and Dev, or just Jake. In the car the prospect thrilled me. Though I wasn't any less aroused, I was beginning to feel a tinge of doubt. Dev was a repressed Dom. For years he'd allowed Jake to be his alpha, this could very well be the first time in years he'd be able to have sex with someone who he could have full control over. What if he went overboard? Or, what if he forced the anal issue? What if--

When I didn't take his coat, but continued staring up at him, he opened the coat closet and set it on a hanger himself. "I'm a bit harsher than Jake, I know that," he began, as though he could read my mind. "If I do anything you don't like, tell me and I'll stop." He held a hand out for my coat, so I squirmed out of it and handed it to him. "Understand? I want you to enjoy being alone with me. I don't want you afraid of me."

After he set my coat in the closet beside his, he advanced. A shiver chilled me when he grasped my chin and angled my head back so he could stare directly into my eyes. "Understand?" he asked again.

"You won't make me have anal sex?"

"I won't do anything you don't want me to do. And don't be afraid to tell me if you're uncomfortable with something. I won't get angry."

Remembering my first time with Jake when he delivered a similar speech, I smiled. "Okay. I understand."

"Good." His hold on my chin tightened and the cold leather gloves sent another chill through my body. As he stood over me, holding me in place, his genial countenance shifted, darkened. Sinister intent was visible in his chocolate gaze. A wicked--or perhaps depraved was a better word--smile appeared on his face. With a free hand he rumpled his waves then gave his head a shake that made his hair tumble around his shoulders in loose curls. Before my eyes he'd transformed himself from Dev into Cinder.

I'd never known anyone as animated as Dev. He was a man who wore every emotion like a badge of honor. Still, seeing his metamorphous from gentle lover to … hell, I had no idea what he'd become, but whatever it was it was turning me on.

"Stella." He spoke in a rich, syrupy voice not entirely his own. It was deep, incredibly sensual, and so sexy I wanted to throw myself at him.

"Dev?"

He shook his head. "Cinder. Take me to your room."

I couldn't explain why thinking of the man before me as Cinder instead of Dev was so arousing, but it was. I could still remember how sexy Dev ... Cinder had looked onstage. He was mesmerizing. Having sex with Dev as Cinder was an exciting surprise.

The moment he released me I nodded and started for the stairs. I'd only gone one step when I remembered the ridiculous outfit I was wearing. The stiletto Mary Jane's, the silly baby doll dress. There was a part of me--an enormous part of me--that felt like a damn fool gallivanting around Maryland in such a getup. But Cinder liked it so I had to at least try to feel sexy in it for him.

Since I knew Cinder had a perfect, unobstructed view of my butt-cheeks peaking beneath the hem of the dress, I made a point to put a little more swoosh in my walk as I ascended to my room.

I could hear him breathing, smell his fruity shampoo in the air around me. The closer I came to my room, the more I realized how desperate I was for Cinder. I loved being with both men, but having Cinder to myself, even if it was only this one time, had been a secret craving I'd never given voice to.

I managed to make it to my bedroom and turn on the lights without fainting from hormonal overload.

This wasn't the first trip to my bedroom Dev had taken, though it was his first when I hadn't anticipated him. Only now, with him at my side surveying my most private space, did I realize how ridiculous my bedroom was.

The simple green and white color scheme was nice, as was my armoire and antique vanity. Even with the various perfumes, makeup, and other girly things scattered along its surface it looked like a nice piece of furniture. What wasn't so nice, what was, in fact, very embarrassing were the various teddy bears I'd collected from ex-boyfriends and piled like pillows on my bed.

I had turned the light on, but quickly turned it off.

Cinder flicked the switch back on then crossed into my room. Trying very hard not to smile, he swept his arm over my bed and sent stuffed toys flying in every direction. When the dust had settled, Cinder was motioning me into the room.

I opened my mouth to explain why this thirty-year-old woman was the owner of, oh, between fifty and sixty stuffed animals but Cinder shook his head. "Don't tell me about your toys. You'll ruin the mood. As it is, I'm hanging by a thread."

Happy to forget the toys, I entered the room. But instead of going to Cinder, I found a box of matches in my nightstand and set about lighting candles. As I moved, Cinder watched, impatience twisting his features unbecomingly. "The overhead light is so harsh," I explained as I moved around the room lighting wicks. "See," I said, once the room was alight with flames. "Isn't that better?"

I returned to the door and turned the overhead light off. Then I jumped when I felt him behind me. He slid his arms around my waist and ground his erection into my lower back. "Are you trying to torture me?" he purred into my ear.

I swallowed hard, wobbled on my feet. "No."

His fingers played along my stomach, tickling a path over me. "Are you ready to be my little sex slave?"

I was ready to be whatever he wanted me to be. "Yes."

"Call me Master, then. Show me how eager you are to submit to me." One thumb stroked the erect nub of my nipple and I moaned at the sudden pleasure. Erotic heat swirled between my legs, my clit throbbed.

He released me.

I turned to him in time to see him step back. He removed his leather gloves and tossed them on the bed behind him. The shirt went next. He unbuttoned it and let it fall to the floor at his booted feet.

Pants and boots remained … and nothing else.

His nipples had puckered. They looked hard as tiny pebbles, and appetizing enough for me to want a taste. I wanted to run my tongue over them, enjoy the feel of the unyielding peaks against my lips.

The sight of Cinder's naked chest had my hormones on full alert. I went to the vanity and subsided into a chair, too aroused to be steady on my feet anymore.

Cinder came forward and hooked his heel on the lowest rung of the chair. "Did I say you could sit?"

"No," I admitted. "I just need a second."

"No, what?" He edged closer, until he was straddling my thighs and standing over me.

I knew what he wanted, so I spread my mouth and forced my lips to form the words. "No, Master."

"Good girl." He gave me an approving pat on the cheek. "Know what I want right now?"

"What?"

He stepped closer, moved nearer until he was pinning my breasts beneath his crotch. I could feel his cock pulsate against me. Even as he stood over me he was growing wonderfully hard.

I chanced a look into Cinder's face as the deliciously decadent sensation of helplessness filled me.

"Undo my pants, beautiful. I want your lips on me."

The air came out of me on a long, uneven sigh. Even as I stared at the growing bulge in his pants I could feel my heart working double time. It couldn't be healthy to get this excited.

"Come on, baby. Show your Master how much you love his dick."

Unsure if I had the mental wherewithal to work the buttons on his pants, I lifted my hands and clasped his waistband.

"Yeah," he encouraged. "That's it."

With more desperation than skill, I yanked the button of his jeans open. It came free with a satisfying *pop*. The upper flaps of his jeans fell open, exposing the dark brown tufts of pubic hair hidden beneath.

"No underwear," I said, stating the obvious.

"Unzip me."

I clasped the warm metal of his zipper and drew it as far down as it would go. As I dragged on the small bit of metal holding his pants together, he rubbed against me. Even before I saw the taut skin of his erection, I felt the hard mass of it as he pressed into me.

"That's it," he said, as I reached into his pants and wrapped my fingers around his girth. I pulled him free as he murmured his appreciation. "Now suck me, kitten. I wanna cum in that luscious mouth."

I had to ease lower in the seat to be on the right level with him. The leather chair let out a muffled squeak as I slid low. I was careful to brace my hands on either side of it for balance. As I got into position, Cinder--who seemed to be getting more aroused by the second--edged closer. His

hands were clenched into such tight fists that his skin had
blanched white. I could hear him panting above me;
breathing so hard his chest was lurching up and down. It
was a little scary to know I was the source of such extreme
emotion. Scary and invigorating. He may be in the
dominant position, but on a far deeper level, I was the one
truly in control.

I chanced a look at him, and then wished I hadn't. Eyes
glazed over with lust and lips set into a determined
grimace, Cinder was a bit scary when he was in such an
advanced state of arousal.

"I'm gonna cum so hard. And I want you to swallow
every bit. Tell me you're gonna swallow every drop of your
Master's cum, Stella."

Weak with desire, I reached for him. Even as I reached,
lifting my head enough to bring my lips into contact with
the silken skin of his cockhead, he leaned in.

When my tongue came into contact with him, he let out a
hiss. "Say it, Stella," he insisted. "Every drop."

"Every drop," I agreed, then closed my mouth over him.

He froze. His hips thrust forward a moment later and the
full length of him slid into the welcoming warmth of my
mouth. Moaning, he began rocking against me.

I lost myself in the feel of his body surrounding me, in the
press of his cock against my tongue. I swallowed him,
bathed him with my tongue. With my hands cupping his
ass, I began to guide him.

At first he allowed me to steer. He seemed so lost in
sensation that all he was capable of was remaining on his
feet. But as his pleasure grew, he took control. His strokes
were deliciously slow at first, but as he neared completion
his movements became faster, more frenzied. With every
thrust he gasped, with every withdrawal I sucked him hard
and ran my tongue over him.

I entwined my legs with the legs of the chair to steady
myself against the powerful motion of his hips, and as I
repositioned, I gazed up. His eyes were intent on me. His
lips parted just enough for me to see his tongue. Then he
gave me a slow, seductive smile.

I think I may have whimpered.

He stared a beat longer and closed his eyes. Lips pursed
and cheeks flushed red, Cinder looked extraordinary.

He gripped the top of the chair and plunged forward, then slowly pulled back. The muscles along his arms were rigid as he moved. Within the confines of my mouth he felt harder. His cockhead had become so large I had to work to swallow it.

"I'm gonna cum," he muttered, too excited to speak clearly.

I squeezed his buttocks, drew him closer and sucked hard, working him with my tongue along his shaft.

He let out a strangled cry, drove in to the root and then spilled his seed inside of me.

"I think I enjoyed that even more than you," I said a few moments later.

Cinder's lids fluttered open and he gave me a glassy eyed stare. "I don't think that's possible."

Still panting from his release, he stroked my face. Then he tucked his softening erection into his pants and backed away from me. He retreated to the comfort of my bed, settling on top of it. Pointing to the floor between his spread feet, he ordered, "On your knees, kitten. Take my boots off."

Coils of heat shifted violently between my legs while a cocktail of erotic need and feminine desire danced within me. I needed Cinder inside me, didn't know if I could stand going another two minutes parted from his body. Nevertheless, I got to my feet.

"On all fours," he said, giving the air between us another jab with his finger.

My heart quickened at his tone. Even as I moved to obey him, my cunt convulsed. I lowered until I was crouching on all fours as ordered.

Though I feared I was fighting a losing battle, I tried my damnedest to school myself to keep eager hands off the pulsing flesh between his thighs. He'd only just climaxed, after all.

Anxious to have the gnawing hunger within me sated, I crawled forward on my hands and knees.

"You look so good, baby." He studied me when I sat back on my knees and stared into his eyes. "What are you waiting for? Take off my boots."

"If I take off your boots will you--"

"You presume to question me?"

"No," I said quickly.

Before he could issue another order, I refocused my attention on said boots. They didn't have any zippers or clasps so I knew to pull them free of Cinder I'd have to grab a hold at the heel and pull. I wouldn't look very sexy hauling biker boots off my man, but it's what he wanted.

I took a deep breath, lowered myself until I was poised inches from his feet, and wrapped my hands around the thick heel. But I didn't pull. I'd meant to pull, but somehow that wasn't what happened.

Gentle as a dove, I bent forward and pressed my lips to the tip of his boot and puckered for a kiss. The soft material was smooth under my lips and the smell of leather engulfed me. I kissed his boot once, then twice, and then I was covering it with soft, wet kisses.

"Shit!" Cinder gasped, sounding suddenly more like Dev. He stiffened and uttered another curse. "Shit, Stella! Don't do that."

My lips were feather soft against him. The scent of leather and man was as potent as any aphrodisiac. Focusing my attention on his other foot, I set my lips to the pliant leather and covered it with adoring kisses as well.

"Stella!" he said again, further losing the smooth indifference he'd had a moment ago. "You can't do that."

But I was doing that. And I wasn't done.

Gripping the heel of his boot in both hands, I gave it a controlled tug and was surprised when it slid easily free of him. His sock was next. It was black of course, and I cast it aside and quickly forgot about it.

"Stella," Dev warned.

Though his tone was stern and his meaning clear--don't do what you're about to do--I decided to ignore him. Had he really wanted me to stop he could easily have pulled free of me. But he didn't. He remained still as stone, staring down at me with a face that had gone stark white. If I weren't so horny I would have laughed at the look of surprise on his face.

Somehow, by giving Dev the kind of total submission he'd always craved, I'd managed to turn the tables on him. I was on my knees at his feet, but suddenly I was the one in control. Dev's need for me to continue made him vulnerable to the point of near helplessness.

Not wanting to completely emasculate him, I focused on his lips from lowered lashes and offered a shy smile. "May I suck your toes, Cinder ... Master?"

Dev groaned. Dragging a hand over his forehead, he made no move to answer. I was about to voice the request again when he sucked in air then slowly expelled it. "Until I tell you to stop," he said, speaking again with Cinder's voice.

When I slid his big toe into my mouth and felt him shudder, I knew it would be a long time before he issued such a dictate.

I sucked him slow, letting my tongue massage every inch of skin with languorous licks that had him squirming on the bed. He tasted faintly of leather and smelled wonderfully of soap. As I laved him I immersed myself in this simple delight.

The longer I remained on my knees, bathing Cinder's foot, the more the lines between master and slave blurred. I wasn't sure who was in control anymore. I was as lost as he was, drowning in my lust even as he floundered for self-control.

When I'd thoroughly savored one foot, I removed his other boot and repeated the process. Cinder went positively mad when I made a wet path over his instep and began sucking on the tender skin.

"Stop," Cinder said. With a fierce tug of his foot, he pulled free of me. "On your feet." Though he strove to sound severe, he was breathing too hard to put enough real venom in his voice. Nevertheless, I got to my feet and stood before him, waiting.

Chest heaving, he let his eyes rove over me. It was a look of total possession. Regardless of my display of momentary control, my knees went weak. Desire made my insides tingle and I had all I could do not to beg Cinder to take me.

Gaining his equilibrium faster than I would have thought possible, he spoke in a low, conversational voice. "I should punish you for that. But I won't. I enjoyed it too much. Have you done that for Jake?"

As quickly as Cinder was taking back control, I was losing it. Feeling at a loss, I focused on my feet.

"Eyes on me. And answer properly."

"No, Master," I said, careful to include the latter word as I knew he wanted.

My answer seemed to amuse him. His lips turned up at the edges and his eyes gleamed wickedly. "Why not?"

I didn't know, so I shrugged.

"You're a perfect sub for Jake and me, you know that? You absolutely love to serve ... that much is evident in the way you throw yourself into the role of submissive."

"I'm not really a submissive," I began to explain, but clamped my mouth shut when he arched his brow.

"Of course you are. Jake knew what he was doing when he found you."

"Is that the only reason you want me?" I blurted, wondering if he felt about me the way Steven did.

Cinder was openly smiling now. "Because you're a sub? Don't be silly. Female subs are a dime a dozen. You'd be surprised how many offers Jake and I get. But you're different, kitten."

"How am I different?"

When he didn't answer, I focused in on his grinning countenance, then gazed lower. Something very interesting had caught my attention.

"Eyes on me," Cinder said, then clasped his zipper a second time today and drew it down. Using one hand, he pulled his engorged length free and then gave me a smile that the anti-Christ would have envied. "Have a seat, Stella."

Chapter Nine

His erection jutted out of his pants, more than ready for me.

On shaky legs, I forced myself toward him. A brief shudder ran through me when he grabbed my hips and slid my dress up until it was around my waist.

Murmuring low, he drew me forward. "Straddle me, baby," he said, hoarsely. "I'm gonna fuck that sweet little cunt."

I let him lead me on top of him. I was careful to spread my knees wide to give him full access. The moment I felt the head of his cock probing my entrance, I sighed. This was what I'd been waiting for. The one thing I'd been hungering for. And now it was happening.

Cinder shifted on the bed, spreading his legs wide while keeping his hands splayed on my hips, guiding me down inch by sensuous inch. "That's it, kitten. Nice and easy."

The slow penetration was a torture. My sex tightened and a deep, rapturous heat began to build in the pit of my stomach. I could feel my abdomen tighten as the luxuriant sensation of being filled washed over me. I bit my lip again, struggled against the nearly overwhelming need to cry out.

I closed my eyes and Cinder lowered me until his full length was buried to the deepest depths of me. He gave his hips a roll and white-hot fire simmered between my legs. "Oh, Cinder."

"This what you want, baby?"

"Yes!" I gasped for breath.

He trailed his fingers over my stomach; let them trace a languid path over the valley between my breasts. Gently palming one in each hand, he squeezed and sucked a nipple into his mouth, then released it. "Are you my good little slave, kitten?"

I nodded. "Don't torture me, Cinder. Please. I can't take it."

He laved the skin at my throat, leaving behind a wet trail that set me to shivering. "Are you?"

"Yes."

When he surged up, then slowly withdrew, I thought my world would stop. Pleasure radiated out to every inch of my body. I writhed in his lap, fought the urge to ride him hard and fast.

"Put your hands behind your back, Stella. Don't move them until I say."

I did as told. It was amazing that something as simple as moving my hands could make me feel so powerless. My arms weren't bound, save Cinder's edict; I was free to move them whenever I chose, yet I felt helpless as a baby.

"I bet you like that, don't you?"

"Yes."

Lust flickered behind his eyes, yet his gaze was steady on me. "Yes what?"

"Yes, Master."

"Say it again. This time with feeling."

Damn the man. "Yes, Master!"

Then Cinder thrust up and into me again.

I screamed in surprised delight. Propelled forward from the driving force of his hips, I tumbled toward him. Pleasure descended on me with blinding force, I shuddered violently.

Lips curled, Cinder stared at me with hungry eyes. Unkempt, rumpled, and disheveled, Cinder had the look of a wild man. And he'd never been sexier than he was at that moment.

He withdrew and surged into me again, bringing a cry of pure feminine delight from me. The rhythm he set was merciless, the sensual thrill, endless. Moving his hips hard and fast enough to have the most decadent sensations uncoiling between my legs, I knew it would be a struggle to keep my orgasm at bay. Meeting him thrust for thrust, already I felt release hovering near.

I felt his hand on the back of my head before I saw him move, felt his fingers on my scalp as he tangled them in my hair and brought my mouth to his.

I met his kiss with a need that matched his. We tasted, licked, nibbled and then he forced my lips wide with his tongue and dove deep. Our lips melded, and I lost myself in the sweet, honeyed flavor that was uniquely Cinder.

"Kitten," he murmured against my lips, sounding like Dev again, "I could fall in love with you." He licked my lips then sucked my tongue into the warmth of his mouth.

He used his free hand on my nipple, plucking it and driving me to the edge of reason. Rolling it between thumb and forefinger, he made me moan.

Abruptly, he pulled back and stared into my eyes. "Promise me this won't be the last time we do this. Just the two of us."

Frantic for release, I nodded. "Fuck me harder, Cinder."

Instead of driving me harder, he slowed. "Promise, Stella. I want to hear you say you promise." He rotated his hips and sent a fresh wave of sensation roiling over me.

"Dear God, Dev, I promise. Anything you want, just fuck me."

Eyes flashing wickedly, he clasped me by the waist and flipped me onto my back.

I sank into the mattress beneath him, reveled in the feel of his body on top of mine.

He reared back, gripped me under the thighs and hoisted my legs over his shoulders. "I'm gonna make you feel good, kitten," he promised through clenched teeth. Then he drove forward.

The previous position had been good, but there weren't words to describe the delicious vibrations humming through my body as he rode me. His cock drove into me hard and sure.

"Cinder," I panted. "Don't stop."

He claimed my mouth, kissing me with a hungry, roving tongue. His mouth was possessive and needy, his taste wonderful.

A sweet climax was building in the deepest recess of my soul, swirling within and demanding release. With every claiming penetration it came nearer, driving me until I was mad with the need for release.

"That feel good, baby?" Cinder asked and plunged into me.

My feet flexed, I screamed. A heady blend of passion and pleasure had me matching him thrust for thrust. Sweat pooled between us, I swiped at a trickle on my cheek.

"Let go, Stella. Cum."

My climax broke over me, sending wave after wave of sweet sensation through me. I shook under the force of it and delighted in the feel of it. Even when Cinder released into me with a loud moan, the spasms continued to race through my body. Only when Cinder lay prostrate and unmoving did the delicious sensations subside.

* * * *

9:33 PM

Two hours later, we were still in my bed. Naked, we had crawled under the covers and cuddled close. I couldn't stop touching him. I touched him everywhere and lost myself in the simple thrill of being close to him. "Tell me," I said again. "I wanna know how you and Jake met."

Dev studied me. His dark eyes seemed to glimmer in the candlelight. "Are there any more Twinkies?"

"No. You ate the last one thirty minutes ago."

"Did I? Are you sure? I can't believe we ate a whole box of Twinkies in two hours."

"Believe it."

Chuckling, Dev rolled onto me and seared me with a hungry kiss. When he rolled away, though, his lips were set in a thin line. "We can't tell Jake about any of this. I don't think he would understand."

"And anyway, nothing we did changes our relationship. Our Triad … that's what Ann calls us."

He moved his thigh over my hip and let it rest there. "Cute."

Our lips touched tentatively, then I squirmed close and we were kissing again, our appetite for each other so strong, I doubted it would ever be sated.

"I can't get enough of you," I said, when we parted again. "See. You have to tell me about you and Jake so I can get my mind off kissing you."

"There's not much to tell. We met when Jake was still a personal trainer at another gym. I'd had an unfortunate accident with a deck--"

"Excuse me?"

Sighing heavily, Dev rolled his eyes. "Who are you now, Barbara Walters? If you must know I was hanging out at a friend's place in Columbia. We were drinking beers on his deck … and a few shots of whiskey." He shrugged. "Guess I had one too many. Somehow I managed to fall off the deck. I broke three fingers in my left hand, my wrist and my arm in two places. And it was my left hand, the hand I used to fret with."

Surprised and horrified, I began to sit up, but Dev wrapped his leg around my waist and held me in place.

"It was six years ago. I assure you, it doesn't hurt anymore. But at the time, it was a bitch. I played lead guitar back then. After I healed up I couldn't get my fretting speed back to where it was before the accident. I did the usual hand exercises, but nothing helped."

"So you started seeing a personal trainer?"

"Yep. And that's how Jake became my personal trainer. That's how we met."

Now I rolled my eyes. "Yeah, but how did you get together?"

Dev snorted, as though this was a stupid question. "Jake decided he wanted me." When I continued to glare, Dev elaborated. "Jake is easily the most beautiful man I've ever seen. Even so, initially I didn't think he was into guys." He smiled at the memory. "Hell, I liked him. I kept up with the training because I liked being around him. He's one of those *hands-on* trainers who likes to get down with the trainee and show them what they're supposed to be doing. He was constantly touching me. I'd leave the gym three times a week with a raging hard-on. But like I said, I didn't know he was into guys. I thought he was touching me because that's how he did his job."

"What happened?"

"He invited me over to his place to watch the O's. I wasn't big on baseball, but you can bet your ass I didn't turn him down. I was so hot for Jake. I'd look at him and practically cum on the spot."

"So what happened," I prodded.

"We're at his apartment. He goes to the kitchen to get more beer … it was a very Jake moment. He's so damn confident. Anyway, I'm sitting on the sofa, cursing myself for being so attracted to a straight guy. I was wondering how I could get out of the situation when Jake comes sauntering into the room with the beer. He sets the beer on the coffee table, all casual, and then he proceeds to straddle me as I'm sitting on the sofa. He looks at me and says, 'You didn't really come here to watch baseball. And I didn't invite you over to watch baseball.' I just gaped."

This story was turning me on. I'd never seen Jake and Dev being intimate without me sandwiched between them. Now I was getting curious. "So what'd you do?"

"I didn't do anything. Jake waited about a millisecond for me to object, and then he kissed me. No, he didn't just kiss me, he devoured me. About a month later I moved out of the three-room apartment I was sharing with the band I was in at the time, and moved in with Jake. And here we are."

Before I could respond, Dev's cell phone began to ring. He rolled away from me and grabbed it off the nightstand. He gave the digital display one look and grinned. "It's Jake."

I sat up.

Dev answered. "What's up? Yeah, I'm dropping Stella off now. No, we didn't buy a dress for the ball, but we got a lot of other stuff you'll like. They're fucking sexy. I guess not. Okay, see you in a few."

Dev disconnected, rolled to face me and kissed me long and slow. "That's from Jake," he said when he was through. "I gotta go."

I watched Dev dress in silence then walked him to the door.

"I had a great time today, kitten." Leaning forward, he gave me a peck on the lips. "Remember. This is our secret. Right?"

I nodded. "Right."

He opened the door, paused. "I had a fantastic time today."

"Me, too."

He edged closer. "I'm glad Jake found you."

"I'm glad I let him find me."

I remained where I was, reclining against the frame of the door, as he bent low, puckered, and gave me a loud, wet kiss on the forehead. "I'm glad I spent the day with you." He kissed my eyelids, brushed his lips over my cheeks, and found my mouth. "I want to be inside you so bad right now, Stella. I can't get enough of you."

I was contemplating pulling him back inside when I heard a voice that made my blood run cold.

"Stella! Girl, what you doing out here in the hall with a …
white man?" My cousin Sadie's voice rose a full octave on
those last two words. She was doing her best guppy
impersonation--mouth wide open and eyes bulging, and
sounding as scandalized as she looked. She stumbled
backward, gripped the railing and held on for dear life. She
was one step shy of tumbling, head over heels, down the
stairs and I was tempted to make my way over just so I
could give her a shove.

Dev arched a brow and darted a questioning look at my
obnoxious cousin.

I groaned. "What are you doing here, Sadie?"

Mindless of the cold, she had braved the nighttime slush
and moisture in a delicate little peach skirt. Her suede coat
was cinched at the waist, and she was wearing three inch
heels. At my harsh demand, she held up a hand, displaying
a pink and white striped Victoria's Secret bag. "Your mom
asked me to bring this over."

Dev and I exchanged a look, and then he pushed away
from me so I could retrieve the proffered bag. "What's in
there?"

Sadie stared at Dev, blinked, then stared some more.

"Sadie! What's in the bag?"

"Oh." She looked me up and down. "Bread. Your mom
made a loaf of banana bread for you."

"And you decided to bring it to me at ten at night?"

Her eyes glided in Dev's direction. "I'm on my way to
Pazo's to meet some friends."

I rolled my eyes. Call me paranoid, but I didn't believe
for one second that she'd come to bring me banana bread at
ten at night, just because she was going out to meet some
friends in Fells Point. She was married and had kids, and it
was Sunday night for crying out loud. "Did my mother
send you here to check up on me?"

Eyes fixed on Dev, Sadie sidled forward.

Though initially she'd been thunderstruck when she'd
seen him, I could tell her interest in him was shifting from
one of shock to one of lascivious female appreciation. As
she approached, her tongue darted out and slithered over
her lower lip. There was a lot of swoosh in her walk now
too, and damned if she wasn't trying to flutter her lashes.
"Are you going to introduce me to your gentleman friend?"

Funny how her speech had gone through a rapid change too. Since when had Sadie been to the south and become a Southern Belle?

"Dev, Cousin Sadie. Cousin Sadie, Dev."

Dev gave me another wet kiss on the forehead, then pushed away from the door, hand outstretched. "Nice to meet you, Sadie."

Sadie dropped the Victoria's Secret bag unceremoniously at my feet, and clutched Dev's hand in both of hers. "I didn't know Stella had a … lover (pronounced, lovaa). She hasn't mentioned any lover."

Argh!

"A minor oversight on her part, I'm sure." Dev pulled free of her then slid his arm around my waist.

"You seem close. Have you been seeing each other for a while?"

"I feel I've known Stella all my life. We're what you'd call, simpatico. Isn't that right, kitten?"

I wondered briefly if he was purposely laying it on thick or if this was his, *meet the family M.O.*

"Oh," Sadie continued, "then you're coming to Stella's birthday dinner?"

Dev paused, glanced at me, frowned.

That idiot! I knew she'd come here with the express purpose of snooping--courtesy of my mom--and to ruin my life.

I hadn't told Dev about the birthday dinner, or Jake, and I hadn't planned on it. My mother, hell, my entire family would not take well to finding out I was dating two men *and* in addition to the fact that there were two of them, neither was black. That just wasn't the kind of thing a girl sprung on her mother. But now Sadie had gone and told Dev and I had to figure out what to do. "Of course he's coming," I said quickly. "Don't be stupid."

"You did tell him about your birthday dinner, didn't you?"

Have I said how much I hate my cousin, Sadie? "I was getting around to it."

Having achieved her night's purpose, she beamed. "Good. I'll just tell auntie--"

"No! I mean, I want it to be a surprise."

Her smile expanded. "Oh." Then, as though she hadn't wreaked enough havoc for one night, she said, "What about Steven? He told me he had a quiet lunch with you here at your apartment the other day. Does he know you're seeing someone?"

At the mention of Steven, the arm around my waist, flexed and tightened.

"Yes. I told him all about Dev." I picked up the bag of bread and started backing into my apartment, careful to pull Dev along with me. "Thanks for stopping by, Sadie. Next time, call first."

Sadie continued to smile. The last thing I saw before I shut and locked the door was Sadie's beaming countenance.

"So who the fuck is Steven?"

I let my forehead smack against the door. Something told me Dev wasn't quite ready to leave yet.

* * * *

10:41 PM

"I'm not seeing anyone else and I'm not ashamed of you," I said.

Crap! And to think I'd been worried he just wanted me for sex.

"Then why didn't I hear about your birthday dinner from you? And why do you have your ex … if he is an ex … coming to your apartment for lunch? And why did I have to hear about these things from a stranger?"

I wanted to curl up on the sofa, close my eyes, and disappear. "Steven is my ex. We dated in high school. I told you why he came over already and it was the truth." And I had told him the truth. "As to the party, it's like I said, I didn't think my mom would understand. In fact, I still don't think she'll understand the fact that I'm seeing two men."

"And that I'm white."

"You know how it is, Dev. It's like with your dad."

"The difference is, I never tried to hide who I am from my father. I'm not ashamed of you or Jake."

"You can't pretend that our relationship is normal."

"So now I'm abnormal."

I wanted to deck Sadie. "No. You're putting words in my mouth."

"Forgive me. What I should have said is that I'm normal, it's just our relationship that's abnormal."

"Stop it, Dev."

"If you're ashamed of us just say it."

"But I'm not ashamed."

Dev's phone rang.

I didn't have to wait for him to answer to know who was on the other line. When he hung up and said, "That was Jake, again."

He uncurled from the loveseat and stood. "I'm gonna head home."

The warmth of the day, the closeness we'd shared, was gone.

Dev went to the door, without waiting for me, and was gone before I'd made it to the foyer.

I hate my cousin.

Chapter Ten

Journal Entry 3/22/05, 4:28 PM

I went to Enoch Pratt today to see how many books I could find about anal sex. Not many. In all honesty, I didn't think I'd find a plethora of anal sex books, but the library is only a few blocks away from my house. I figured I might as well give it a go. I'm also thinking that a gift of anal sex might soften Dev after the other night.

I haven't spoken with him all day.

I hate Sadie Rice. The cow!

In any case, after Pratt I rang up Ann, hoping to get her before she left my apartment for the day. I convinced her to give me a ride to the Barnes and Noble bookstore by the harbor.

You know, for such a large bookstore, B&N didn't have a very big section on sexuality. I managed to find a few books, though. But I refuse to write the titles down here where they'll be present for all eternity for anyone who happens upon my journal. That would be too embarrassing. Let's just say that the sum total of all I learned isn't much more than what Ann and Meagan already told me. Push against the prick when it's going in and relax. I'm fifty bucks poorer and that's essentially all I learned.

* * * *

Journal Entry 3/24/05, 12:02 PM

I was sprawled across my living room sofa, Coke with lime in hand and my telephone balanced on my shoulder as I listened and took sips from the nearly empty glass.

"Why don't you come over tonight?"

"I don't know, Dev."

Dev breathed for a few moments, each exhalation of air peppering the transmitter in staccato bursts. "Jake wants to see you."

"What about you? Are you still pissed?"

Again, Dev was silent for a few beats. "No."

"So we're cool?" I stood and went to the window, stared two floors below at a small crowd gathered across the street, snapping pictures at my neighbor's row house. Tourists.

"We're fine, Stella. So are you coming over or not?" Dev said in a rush, as though talking to me was suddenly inconveniencing him.

"It doesn't sound like we're fine."

"But we are."

"Are you sure?"

"What the fuck ... ? Do you want me to send you an engraved invitation? Are you coming over or not?"

I heard movement at the other end of the line and pictured Dev lounging in front of the fireplace in his living room, legs outstretched on the coffee table as he glared into the flames.

"No, I'm not coming over, you ass."

Another exhale. "All right, fine." He paused. "You're still going to the masquerade ball, right?"

The nerve! If he thought he could act like a prick then expect me to go out with him, he had another thing coming. "Why the hell should I? Just to have you act like an ass all night because you're stupid enough to believe my stupid cousin?"

"I don't believe her. I know you didn't do anything with that guy ... that Steven."

"Then why are you acting like--" I considered, and then found an appropriate description, "--like a little bitch."

Dev was silent. For a moment I feared I'd pushed him too far. Then, he sucked in air, and laughed. "Little bitch? Did you just call me a little bitch?"

"You heard me."

He continued to chuckle, laughing a bit even when he started talking again. "I'm jealous, kitten. Can't you see that? And it pisses me off."

"Jealous of what?"

"That you had your ex-lover over. That he was in your home, with you. Alone."

"Not alone. Ann was here."

"Nevertheless, I'm jealous. I don't like thinking about you with any man other than Jake and me. There, I said it. Are you happy now?"

I leaned against the window, smiling to myself. "Yes. And as to the ball, I'm still coming."

The line fell quiet. When he spoke again, his voice was rich with innuendo. "Not yet, kitten ... but you will be."

* * * *

Journal Entry 3/26/05, 10:07 PM

"It was amazing." I paused to beam at the girls. Though I was trying not to look smug, it was difficult. "The downside is that I feel like I've cheated on Jake with Dev, even though the three of us are in a relationship together. Having two boyfriends is really confusing."

I was poised on the edge of a fat red pillow at our five hundred dollar a month table--The Tower--eating calamari and working on my second Sam Adams of the night. The Mediterranean décor of The Tower combined with good beer and my memories of Dev were giving me an emotional high. I knelt at the low table with my knees pressing into the plush pillow. The sheer red, gold and purple draperies hanging from the walls made me think of Jake's bed, which of course made me think of Dev and our wonderful day together. The flickering candles surrounding our table were a constant reminder of the candles I'd lit for Dev and me.

I sighed. Dev was amazing. And that he was capable of jealously! Adolescent though it was, I was thrilled that Dev had been jealous of Steven.

Ann, Katarina, and Meagan stared at me, matching looks of irritation on their faces.

Mayhap I did look a little too pleased with myself. I sure as hell felt pleased with myself.

Glowering at me over a plate of hot wings, Meagan was the first to speak. "If you're looking for someone to feel sorry for you, hon, you're in the wrong place with the wrong people. I refuse to feel sorry for anyone who gets as much sex as you do these days."

Stealing a hot wing from her dish, I picked succulent bits of meat from the bone and popped them into my mouth. "You're missing the point," I said between chews. "I don't want sympathy. I want to know if it's cheating to have sex with Dev behind Jake's back."

Sitting diagonally across from me, Ann finally looked to be giving the question serious consideration. "I say no."

Beside me, Katarina rolled her eyes. "That's a surprise?"

"Just listen," Ann continued. "I'll explain. You have sex with Jake when Dev's not around, right Stella?"

I nodded. "Right."

"And you can bet your soon to be de-virginized ass that Jake and Dev fuck like rabbits when you're not around.

I grunted.

Truth was I hated the idea of Jake and Dev doing anything when I wasn't around except longing for my presence. In my favorite fantasy, I thought of Jake and Dev as very sexy robots. Man-bots! When I went to their house, the force of my presence powered them and gave them life, but the moment I left them, they retreated into a sort of stasis, which they would remain in until I returned.

Aren't fantasies great!

"So what's the big deal if you and Dev screw around without Jake?" Ann was saying. "You're a triad. You can't cheat when you're in a triad."

I fingered a bit of calamari, contemplating what Ann had said. She had a point. "I suppose you're right."

Beside me, Katarina's blonde tresses bounced around her head as she shook it. Ann eyed her over the bottle of MGD she was holding. "You disagree?"

"No, I think you're right," Katarina said, "but right or wrong has nothing to do with it. You don't know Jake. The man's on a serious power trip. If he finds out Stella and Dev had sex behind his back, he'll be pissed. Jake isn't the kind of guy who's accustomed to--" she stared up at the ceiling, lips pursed and eyes narrowed. "Defiance," she decided. "That's the best word. I bet it's the word Jake would use. That, or maybe disobedience."

Katarina wasn't helping. I'd felt comforted by Ann's assertions, reassured by her justifications, but Katarina had gone and shot my guiltless outlook to shit. And she was scaring the crap out of me. Defiance? Disobedience? "You make Jake sound like Pol Pot."

"You and Dev are the one's trying to sneak around behind his back."

"What sneaking? There's no sneaking. It was a one time deal."

"All right," Ann agreed. "I'll have to throw my lot in with Katarina. Don't tell Jake."

Meagan stared at me for a moment, a slow smile forming. "Unless, of course, you want him to paddle that ass again."

All righty, time to change the subject.

Despite the uproarious laughter of my turncoat friends, I affixed my *holier than thou* expression to my face and ignored them.

When they quieted enough for me to be heard, I gave a go at starting a new conversation. "When are you gonna tell us what happened with Peter? We've been waiting all night."

Ha! The amusement slid off Meagan's face in a millisecond. It was like watching wax melt. Feeling smug yet again, I shifted on the pillow and stole another hot wing.

Jumping on the bandwagon with both feet, Ann twisted around to look at Meagan and added, "Yeah!" to my request.

"I've been thinking about you and Peter all day," Katarina said. "Tell us what happened when you confessed your undying love to him."

Wide-eyed, Ann stared at Katarina for a few seconds. "Tell us, Meagan, before Miss Mary Sunshine over there starts spewing more of that saccharine crap."

"You're about to be married, Ann, and you're about as romantic as a boar."

"And fucking proud of it." Ann hoisted her MGD and toasted herself.

"Marriage is wasted on you. Romance is wasted on you. You'd be happy enough to live out the rest of your life by yourself."

"Meagan?" I prodded, desperate to end this *discussion* before it really got going.

Ann set her beer on the table and leered at Katarina. "Better to live my life by myself than spending it clinging to the bootstrap of some man I hooked up with just so I wouldn't be alone."

Katarina's mouth fell open. She began to sputter.

"Meagan," I said through clenched teeth. "Tell us about Peter."

For a moment, Meagan looked mutinous. But when the alternative was refereeing a verbal catfight between Ann and Katarina, there was only one choice to make.

With Katarina in mid-sputter, Meagan began. "I chickened out. Happy now? I got to his place and I couldn't do it."

Shit! From one crisis to the next.

Katarina turned and Ann transferred her attention from Katarina to Meagan. "You what?" Ann demanded.

"Chickened out."

"But you got a negligee for the occasion, and sexy panties. How could you chicken out?"

I didn't see the correlation between undergarments and a confession of love, but decided to leave it alone. "Did he do something?"

Fingering the bright pink, blue, and yellow parasol poking from her Margarita, Meagan frowned. "I was at his place, he'd made dinner and we were drinking wine … everything was perfect."

"So what happened?"

"I got the jitters. I started thinking, what if he turns me down? What if he's not interested in having a relationship with me? I don't think I could take that kind of rejection, Stella."

Okay. This was a new twist. How on earth could gorgeous Meagan be afraid of rejection? For the twenty-five years we'd been friends I'd never, not once, seen or heard of any breathing male turning her down.

Elbows flat on the table with her chin resting on a fist, Katarina looked as confused as I felt. "But you ask guys out all the time. You never worried about rejection before."

Continuing her intent study of the tiny, multi-colored umbrella, Meagan shrugged. "It's different with Peter. We've been seeing each other off and on for about a year now. He says no, and that's it for us."

"If he doesn't want to be in a serious relationship you can't go back to things the way they were?" I asked. "The way they are now?"

Meagan shook her head. "I'd be too humiliated."

"But that's crazy," Katarina said. "Peter's a great guy. If he doesn't want to be in a relationship now, give it a few months. He may change his mind. Why throw everything away just because your ego's been bruised?"

"This isn't about my ego, Katarina."

"Yes it is. You're too petrified to take a chance on a sure thing because you're afraid you'll be hurt. Well at long last, welcome to the real world where rejection is possible and not every man is dying for a chance to fall at your feet."

The table went silent.

I was still staring at Katarina, completely caught off guard when a feminine voice I vaguely recognized as Ann's began speaking. "The other guys were just guys, Katarina. Don't you understand that? If she asked out some guy she thought was hot and he turned her down, big deal. Who the fuck cares? But Peter isn't just some guy, he's the man Meagan's in love with. You can't just tell the man you're in love with how you feel and not be afraid. There's a lot more than ego on the line. Meagan's about to offer Peter her heart ... I think he'll take it, but if he doesn't--" Ann grimaced. "You don't just bounce back from a broken heart, Katarina. It can't be done. So if you're gonna offer your heart to someone, you better be damn sure they want it."

Who the hell was this person and what had she done with Ann? "You and Gerard didn't break up again did you?" I asked.

Ann waved the question off. "No. But I remember how I felt last month. Last month sucked." She paused for a beat then smiled. "Until he proposed to me. And we still haven't decided on a date, so don't ask."

After two years of dealing with Ann's indecision, Gerard had broken up with her last month. Subsequently, Ann spent February either drinking, crying, or plotting against Gerard's new girlfriend. In the end, they both realized how important the other was and got back together. Gerard had proposed ... Ann had accepted, and all was good again. But for a while, things had been rocky for Ann.

Katarina ran her fingers through her hair and sat back. "I'm sorry." She shook her head, seemed as confused by her outburst as we were. "I'm sorry," she said again. "Bad day."

Eyes on Katarina, Meagan took a sip from her glass. "Wanna talk about it?"

"Not particularly. Tell me more about the beach house."

She gave Katarina's hand a squeeze, and then released her. "I wanted to talk to you about the beach house anyway."

Katarina perked up. "Did you find one?"

"Yep. In Rodanthe. It's a relatively quiet town but still good for what you have in mind. Ocean views galore, and very romantic. I think you'll like it."

"Ooh! Tell me more."

"It's on the ocean, just like you wanted. There are a few houses around it, but each house has a two-acre lot, so they're not right on top of each other. There's a Jacuzzi, a sauna, an indoor gym--supposedly state of the art, a gourmet kitchen with two ovens, a slew of amenities, a reading room--"

Katarina's lip curled. "Last thing I plan to do is read. It sounds fantastic Meagan. I can't wait." She was positively glowing now. I could almost see the visions of traipsing around on the sandy beaches with Jim flashing in her mind's eye. "How much?"

"And it has five bedrooms, did I say that already?"

"Sounds wonderful, Meagan," I agreed. "I can't wait."

"How much?" Ann asked.

"The kitchen's really big. The house is huge. One of the biggest in Rodanthe."

Katarina's smile vanished. A tiny worry line appeared between her furrowed brows. "Why so big?"

Meagan smiled wide. The fakest damn smile I'd ever seen. "That's the other thing I wanted to tell you guys about tonight. I didn't tell Peter I'm in love with him, so he was wondering what it was I had to tell him that was so important."

"And," Katarina prodded, deadly serious now.

"And I sort of invited him to the beach house."

"You what?" Katarina demanded, just as Ann was saying, "Well if Peter and Jim are going, I'm inviting Gerard."

And thus, we all agreed to ask our boyfriends to take a vacation with us next month, much to Katarina's chagrin.

Chapter Eleven

Journal entry 3/27/05, 5:33 PM

Going to Jake and Dev's tonight. Have no idea what I should wear.

* * * *

6:03 PM

Have showered and am doing my hair. Still have no idea what I should wear.

* * * *

6:43 PM

Hmmm. Wonder if we're going to have sex as soon as I get there. If so, clothing is irrelevant since I won't be dressed long.

* * * *

7:33 PM

In Ann's car now. Figured she could have a look at me to see if I met muster.
Oh Crap, we're here.
Later!

* * * *

7:41 PM

I arrived on the scene unsure of what to expect.
I absolutely wasn't prepared for what I got.
Jake appeared on the doorstep dressed in clinging blue spandex shorts. His hair was pulled into a ponytail and held in place at the nape of his neck. Nipples, blushed a rosy pink, were on a level with my face and the turgid peaks told me Jake was already well on his way to arousal.
He looked amazing.
"Ah, Stella," he said by way of greeting. "I missed you." He pulled me into an embrace. His body was nice and

Adrienne Kama

warm. Being there with him, in his arms, was too perfect for words.

"I missed you too," I said against his chest.

After a moment, he pulled back and stared at me. "It's like I haven't seen you in weeks instead of days."

I managed to keep from giggling like an idiot female. Instead, I endeavored to look cool, yet pleased with his pronouncement, and added, "Me too," while giving him a squeeze. "I missed you both."

"Since it's been a while for us, Dev and I planned something … fun for the evening. I think you'll like it."

I slid a finger in the waistband of his pants and tugged. "I suppose that's why you're wearing blue spandex?"

Pulling my finger free, he held my hand and shut and locked the door.

I followed him up the spiral staircase to the bedroom he and Dev shared, wondering the entire time if I'd again managed to get myself in over my head. *Something fun* could be anything. I could never guess what sex game Jake and Dev had planned because they were far kinkier than I'd ever been.

Then I had a thought. What if they'd decided tonight was the night for anal play? I wasn't ready for the anal thing? "Anal sex?" I muttered, feeling incredibly stupid.

"Nope. The day we do that, it'll be your choice." He stopped at his bedroom door and pushed it open.

I hadn't been there in days, yet the mahogany four-poster, the focal point of the room, was as familiar to me as my own bed. There was a fire blazing in the fireplace opposite the bed, as always, so the room was nicely warm.

What I hadn't been expecting, however, was that rather than filling the room with candlelight the way he usually did, Jake had turned on every light. The space was ablaze with illumination.

Jake turned to me. His eyes on me were like a caress, lingering for long moments at my breasts. It was as intense as a touch and I found my body was awakening sexually as I stood.

The mere act of being in a bedroom with Jake made me so hot that I thought my blood might start to boil. With his smooth, bare chest and ripped body, Jake was positively lethal on the eyes.

His lips were slightly open and I caught a small movement at the edge of his mouth. The skin there seemed to move of its own accord, bunching and loosening at quick intervals. I realized suddenly that Jake was trying very hard not to smile.

He turned from me, and walked further into the room, moving with the kind of male pride that said he knew he was the focus of all eyes. "Come in Stella, I want to play with you for a while."

I let my eyes follow the path he'd made across the room, and then gaped. "Do what?" I demanded, eyeing the object at his feet.

In response, he stepped into a very large, very blue kitty pool and met my gaze. His emerald eyes gleamed with wicked intent. "I want to play with you. In here."

"In the kitty pool!"

His smile broadened. "Don't pretend you're not turned on."

"If I get in, what are you gonna do to me?"

Jake shrugged. "Just a little wrestling match. I won't hurt you."

I took a step back.

"Stay, kitten. I promise you'll enjoy this."

For the first time since entering the bedroom, I realized Jake and I weren't alone. Dev, who was reclining on the bed--how had I missed him--had a look of avid expectation on his face. His lips quivered as his eyes danced from Jake to me and back again. Dressed in his signature leather pants and silk shirt, Dev's expression could only be described as devious. Already there was a large bulge forming in the crotch of his pants. As I stared at his hardening cock, Dev let his fingers trail the length of his thigh. Gently, he stroked his hard on. His fingers moved languidly over the leather encased mound as I stared. He cupped himself and a frisson of pleasure stole over me. Butterflies flapped silken wings in my stomach and began to dance. My cunt gave a hungry clench and I had to bite my lower lip to keep from moaning. "What's going on, Dev?"

"A wrestling match," Dev explained. "Or rather I should say, a Jell-O wrestling match. Go ahead. Have a look inside."

I made my way across the room, careful to keep my eyes on Jake in case he made any sudden movements, and Dev continued to speak.

"This isn't a match of dominance, kitten. Jake would obviously have the upper hand if it was, just a bit of fun. He won't hurt you." I twisted round to look at Dev in time to see him brush invisible dust from his leather pants. Clearly interested in my thoughts on the kitty pool, he sat upright. "This match is to be a more inventive sort of match. The loser will still be the first to submit to the victor, but when I say submit I mean sexually submit."

Standing mere inches from the kitty pool, I glanced at the mounds of Jell-O within.

I had to admit, if only to myself, that Jake knew me too well. I was willing to wager this "contest" had been his idea. He'd know the mere thought of wrestling in Jell-O to sexual submission would turn my insides to mush.

This wasn't exactly fair. Nevertheless, I stripped down to my pink Victoria's Secret boy shorts and bra, stepped over the edge of the pool, and forced thoughts of what Ann, Katarina, and Meagan would say if they knew what I was doing.

Jell-O wrestling! How could this be my life?

* * * *

8:01 PM

"I told you she'd like this," Jake informed Dev. "Look at her."

"I am," Dev said from his position on the bed. "If she doesn't hyperventilate before you get your hands on her I'll consider this a success. Are you all right, kitten?" Dev went on. "You're not going to have a heart attack or anything, are you? I'd never forgive myself."

Though he'd said it with a teasing tone, I thought I just might have a heart attack at that. Was it healthy to be so turned on? Jake hadn't even touched me and already I felt close to climax.

The heat that had teased a few moments earlier had turned into an inferno. Heat scorched, making me near on desperate to throw myself at Jake's feet and beg him to get on with things.

Jake, in stark contrast, stood cool and motionless. His eyes were fixed to my face, though he allowed them to dip lower every few seconds. I could feel his gaze on my breasts, my thighs, and my naked legs. Although he gave no indication that he was suffering as much as me, his cock was steadily growing hard.

"You like that?" Jake asked, seeing where I was looking. He cupped his erection and squeezed.

My eyes crossed.

For a moment I gazed adoringly at Jake, mindless of the fact that I was doing precisely what he wanted me to do. Then a loud *ding* broke me out of my reverie. I hopped into the air and let out a chirp of surprise.

Grinning, Jake lowered himself until he was on his knees and then waited.

When I made no move toward him he motioned me forward with a flick of his index finger. "It'll be fairer if I start on my knees."

And it was. For about two seconds.

I'd barely taken three steps when I found myself flat on my stomach, cherry Jell-O squashed beneath my breasts, with my arms folded in some complicated submission hold behind my back. Jake lay across my supine form, the weight of his body more than enough to keep me pressed to the mat beneath him.

His chest heaved against my back, but more than that, his cock pressed insistently into my backside, drawing me ever closer to the point of no return. The heat of his body enveloped me, leaving me hard pressed to inhale without taking in the delicious scent of him. He smelled wonderfully of man and soap, and it was all I could do not to give up right there and then. What kept me from doing just that was the realization that he was really wrestling me.

Being flat on my stomach with my arms twisted behind my back was enough of an indicator that Jake was using an honest to God, true-blue wrestling hold to subdue me, or at least it felt like one. I was completely immobile.

"This isn't fair," I complained around a mouth full of Jell-O.

"What's not fair? Am I hurting you?"

I considered. "Well, no. But you're using real wrestling moves."

"Am I?"

"You know you are." My voice began to sound shallower as the press of his weight made it increasingly difficult to speak. "I thought this was supposed to be a seduction."

A sudden wetness against my cheek had me struggling to turn over. Unfortunately, Jake's weight kept me in place. With me motionless he was able to run his tongue leisurely over my throat as I shivered helplessly at every contact. "I love cherry," he said, then released me.

I rolled to the right then scuttled to my knees and scurried to the opposite end of the pool. When I turned and sat on my butt, I saw Jake was crouched on his knees, a wicked grin on his face.

Rather than watching me, Jake located Dev's new perch-- on the floor beside the pool--and focused on him. "I thought you were going to buy lime."

Dev, who was darting glances from me to Jake, looked on the verge of climbing into the pool himself. His breathing was coarse and even shallower than my own. His shirt hung open and his nipples were hard as pebbles.

"They were out," he said, breathlessly. "Get on with it, Jake."

Jake settled his hands on his hips and smiled broadly. "In a rush, are we?"

"Do you see her ass in those panties? Hurry up and make her submit so we can have fun."

Jake glanced at me, then back at Dev. "When I'm ready."

Only then did I realize that not only was this exercise meant to torment me, but it was for Dev's benefit as well. It was an agony for him to watch his lovers rolling around, half-naked, knowing he couldn't take part.

Somehow, Jake had gotten control of things, as usual.

I was biting my lip, trying to figure out how he'd done it when a hand closed around my ankle and pulled.

I let out a yelp of surprise. My arms wind milled as I sought something to grab hold of. I sprawled on my back and cherry Jell-O went flying. Even as I was dragged toward the center of the pool, I scrambled to find some sort of grip where I could get a hold and right myself.

"You win, Stella," Jake was saying. "No more wrestling moves. You're right. That's not fair."

Even as he spoke he released my ankle and began to slither up my body. His hair, which had begun coming loose, tickled my bare skin as he moved. His biceps bulged with every motion, his muscles flexing as he continued to crawl up my prostrate form. When we were face to face, he settled himself and grinned.

Caged in his arms and as immobile as before, I merely grunted when he asked, "Better?" Still grinning, he rotated his hips so his rigid dick ground against my clit. "How about now?"

I swallowed the sigh threatening to escape me. My legs trembled. I was desperate for a coring and I was willing to wager Jake knew it.

"I want to fuck you so bad, Stella, I can hardly think straight," he said, no doubt to torment me further. "Do you want me to fuck you, baby?"

Yes, yes, and yes! But I said, "Not particularly."

Jake threw his head back and laughed. "You're gonna make me work for this, aren't you?" he said, seeming pleased by the prospect.

"I've no idea what you're talking about."

"Is that so?" When he moved this time, it was to mold his cock to my clit and rock against me. The movement was slow, deliberate, and so good I nearly begged him to take me then and there.

A rush of sensations took hold of my body at once, the most intense of these coming from the juncture of my thighs where I needed him most. I bucked helplessly as my body's need to be sated overrode my mind's desire for calm. Even as he rubbed, the extra friction of my panties making his movements unbearable, I had all I could do not to cry out. As it was, I moaned and twisted beneath him. No matter how I turned though, I couldn't escape his delicious torment.

"What were you saying, Stella?"

I sighed.

"What was that? Did you say you give?"

Needing to feel his body against mine I reached for him. I didn't care if we were lying on mounds of Jell-O. But, he was wet with sweat and my hands slid over his damp skin. Instead of gripping his shoulders as I'd planned, my reach was off and I got two handfuls of armpit.

Jake let out a surprised gasp and bucked. "Stop it!"

I tried to pull him toward me. Problem with that was my hands were still lodged in his armpits.

He squirmed, giggled, then squirmed some more.

Realization dawned. Oversized, kickboxing, domineering, Jake was ticklish.

Seeing this development for what it was--a chance to even my odds--I happily took advantage before he could roll away. I flexed my fingers and tickled, mercilessly.

"Stop!" he called out again, then threw himself to my left.

A bizarre wresting match ensued, with Jake trying to get free of my busy fingers. He rolled around in the Jell-O, but like a flea on a dog, I would not be shaken free. I clung to him, wrapping my legs around his waist and holding on for dear life as Jake bucked, twisted, giggled, and howled for mercy.

If only I had a camera to capture this moment on film. I'd watch the clip over and over and over again.

Jake said something like, "Do something." And I knew he wasn't talking to me. I could only assume this demand was issued to Dev.

"That's cheating," Dev managed from somewhere behind me.

It was then that common sense returned to Jake. Much to my chagrin, he stopped rolling when he was on top of me, and then simply let his weight fall.

The surprise of having all two hundred plus pounds of Jake atop me was enough for me to release a gasp and loosen my tickle hold. There was no squirming out of his reach now. In short order he caught hold of my wrists and levered them over my head. Though we'd been rolling around in the stuff, the Jell-O felt cold against the back of my hands as he pressed them firmly against the floor of the pool.

Panting, Jake's emerald gaze pinned me to the spot as effectively as his body. "You little hellion, you're gonna pay for that." He looked up, his eyes moving around the room until he found Dev. "Come here, Dev."

Dev, who was busy swiping tears from his cheek, climbed over the edge of the pool then crouched on his knees beside Jake. He chuckled once and then seemed to get himself under control.

The sight of his leather-sheathed legs against the red Jell-O was so indescribably sexy, I thought I might do something stupid at any moment. Seeing the two of them side-by-side made me feel a little light-headed. I should have been annoyed Jake had captured me, but I wasn't. Especially not if what I'd done had led him to get Dev involved.

"Hold her down," Jake said, nodding in the direction of my already pinioned arms.

Dev needed no further prompting. He crawled until he was stationed behind my head, grinning to himself as he went. "My pleasure."

A moment later I felt the press of Dev's knees against my elbows. I knew then that I was fully caught. With over half of each arm captured beneath Dev's body, I'd be there until he decided to release me.

"What a bad little girl you are," Jake began.

"This is cheating," I said. "And it's not fair."

Unfazed, Jake shrugged. This small movement sent a ripple of muscular activity off in his arms and broad shoulders. "Who said I was fair?" He clasped the edge of my bra between his fingers. "I'm gonna make you beg me to fuck you, Stella." He shoved at the cup of my bra until my left breast tumbled free of the constricting material. For long moments he merely stared at the exposed flesh.

Above me, I could hear Dev's harsh breathing. "Isn't she beautiful?"

Jake didn't answer; instead he began a slow, torturous teasing. Ruthlessly, he pinched the nub of my breast until it was stiff and tickled the sensitive peak with unhurried strokes of his fingers. "Is this better, Stella?"

I didn't answer. I couldn't. I was too turned on. Luscious sensations were flowing through my body. I rocked helplessly, fought to maintain my composure.

"And this?" he said, shoving at the other cup of my bra. But he didn't touch that breast. Instead, he looked away.

The pressure on my arms increased as Dev began to move. No doubt he and Jake had shared some silent exchange.

My thoughts were proven true when Jake released me so Dev could cup a breast in each hand and begin kneading. "Does that feel good, kitten?" he wanted to know.

It did. And I wanted more.

Jake's eyes fixed to the leisurely movement of Dev's fingers. "She's so responsive, isn't she?" Jake said.

"That's what I love about her."

Dev exerted force on my nipples, squeezing gently until I was sure I'd go mad. I threw my head to the left and right and squirmed. I didn't know how much more I could take. I needed a release, an end to my suffering.

As if seeing my torment and sorry for it, Jake stroked my face. He drew a finger over my fluttering eyelids, down my cheek, and ran it over my lips. Mindless of what I was doing, I drew his finger into my mouth and sucked.

This seemed to please Jake. "Tell me you want me, Stella."

Aroused, but no less hard-headed, I shook my head in denial.

He worked his finger, slipping it in and out of my warmth as I licked and sucked. "I'll end your torment right now. All you have to do is tell me you want me."

Dev pinched my nipples again, driving me to the brink of sanity. "Go on, kitten, say it."

Again, I shook my head.

Jake gazed at me. For a moment I was terrified he'd order Dev to stop, but that didn't happen. Jake pulled his finger free of my mouth--that wicked half-grin fixed to his face. Making Dev stop seemed the furthest thing from his mind.

"One last chance."

"No," I managed.

Before I had time to prepare myself, Jake's arm disappeared between us. I felt the heat of his skin against my stomach as his hand burrowed beneath the band of my boy shorts. My freshly waxed mound tingled as his fingers casually moved over my naked flesh. His touch was deliberate, meant to tease. But a moment later the teasing had ended. He found my clit and tickled.

Though both men had me pinned beneath them, my back arched and I screamed. The sudden movement caught them both off guard. Even as I writhed, twisting one way then the other, Dev was struggling to maintain his position.

When Jake slid a finger into me I called his name. Pride was forgotten as pleasure came at me. Sensations radiated from my slit out to every part of my body. The pleasure was sharp, intense, and so good I thought I'd climax from the sheer force of it.

I felt Dev's weight lift for a moment, felt him force my arms down before I could get free of him, then his knees were there again, pressing my elbows to the floor. His leather-sheathed thighs caged my head, and his crotch pressed firmly against my crown. His delicious scent mingled with Jake's, the commingled aroma of both men driving my need to fever pitch.

Jake continued his erotic play. He eased his finger inside, penetrating me while his thumb flicked my clit. "You like that?" He asked, as he did it again.

I couldn't take anymore. This was too much. Too much sensation. Even as Dev stroked the tight bud of my nipple, Jake slid two fingers into my wet depths. Before Jake began speaking again, I was ready to admit defeat.

"Tell me you want me, Stella," he said, his expression grim. "Say it and I'll make you cum so hard you'll never want to part from me again."

Fingers deep inside, Jake tickled.

I bucked wildly, twisted uncontrollably. My entire body had become a sensor of pleasure. "I want you, Jake," I screamed.

Jake's lips twitched, but he suppressed his smile. "How much do you want me, Stella?"

As he said this, he slid his fingers from me.

"No!"

"How much do you want me, Stella?"

Obviously taking his cue from Jake, Dev released me as well. Though he was panting heavily, he was doing far better than I was.

I stared at Jake, disbelief making me want to cry out. I wanted to make him finish what he'd started, wanted to make him slide his fingers into my wet cunt and make me climax. But more than his fingers I wanted his cock. I could feel the girth of it pressing into my thigh.

Resting his hands on the floor, Jake said again, "Tell me how much you want me, Stella."

I dragged my tongue over parched lips and sought control. If I didn't tell Jake what he wanted to hear he was likely to leave me suffering for the rest of the night. "I want you," I began slowly, hoping that all Jake needed to hear was something that would stroke his ego, "so much it hurts."

Jake raised a brow. "You're gonna have to do better than that."

What did the man want from me? My unborn children? "I want you more than I've ever wanted any other man I've been with."

This brought a grin to Jake's lips. "Now we're getting somewhere. You say more than any other man you've been with ..." he paused, waiting for a response. His grin broadened into a smile. "Does that include Dev?"

That stopped me cold. Damn it all. I'd walked right into that one. How could I answer that question?

I let my eyes rest on Jake, on the slow rise and fall of his chest and the disheveled hair against his shoulders. Then I looked up until I could see Dev. "I want you both the same."

Jake stared at me for a moment and his expression changed. "I think it's time for dinner."

"What?" Dev and I said in unison.

"I'm hungry." That said, he rolled away, got to his feet and went to his dresser. As he pulled a pair of jogging shorts from within, he continued to speak. "Would you mind starting dinner while I shower, Dev? Stella, you can shower in the bathroom down the hall." He crossed the room, entered the bathroom, and shut the door.

Dev and I were frozen. I couldn't believe what had just happened.

When the shower came on I realized Jake wasn't kidding. He was finished.

"Dev?" I asked, hoping he'd do something to take the edge off my arousal.

Dev got to his feet. "I can't. He wants to save it for later. Go on and shower, I'll be downstairs."

"But I don't want to wait."

"You won't have to wait long."

Damn! Damn! Damn!

I lay in the pool long after I heard Dev's footfalls recede down the hall. I was too horny to get up and retreat. There was no way I could even think about eating in my present state. Talk about cruel and unusual punishment.

The thought of punishment had me sitting upright.

At nearly thirty-one years old I was far too old to be subject to arbitrary punishments. Who did Jake think he was to get up and stroll out of the room while I was horny? I wanted sex, damn it! And I didn't think I should have to wait until Jake decided I deserved it.

Setting my jaw, I got to my feet with one thought in mind. If I wanted sex there was nothing wrong with going and getting it. The only question that remained was from what source I should go to. Dev was cooking dinner down in the kitchen and Jake was naked in the shower. The choice seemed obvious.

Chapter Twelve

9:37 PM

I closed my hand around the bathroom doorknob, twisted, and edged the door open a crack. Despite my resolve to take what I wanted from Jake, I was terrified. I'd never done anything like this before. The thought that he might reject my advances froze me to the floor just outside the door for a good ten seconds.

White billows of steam flowed through the open door and the moist air within dampened my face. The room within smelled sweetly of Zest soap and apple scented shampoo, two aromas I would associate with Jake for the rest of my life.

An image of Jake in his too tight spandex shorts flashed in my mind's eye, deciding me. I was going in.

Cautious not to make any noise, I slid through the narrow opening in the doorway and shut the door behind me. I thought briefly about locking it but decided against it. Dev was the only other person who might enter and I wasn't opposed to that.

My eyes fluttered furiously as hot steam rose around me. I had to blink repeatedly before they became accustomed. Though there were enough lights in the bathroom to light a bowling alley, Jake only used one. The dim light above the commode. Still, despite the hazy mist, I had a perfect view of the sunken bathtub on the far side of the room, the commode, the sink, and the shower stall where a very naked, very wet Jake was rinsing shampoo from his hair.

Again, I stood stiff as a board, mentally gearing myself up for what I was about to do. All I had to do was be confident and insistent … and sexy. What naked man could resist a half-naked, thoroughly aroused woman--covered in Jell-O-- who wanted nothing more than to have sex with him?

Jake could very well be that man. But I wouldn't know until I tried.

Taking a deep breath, I forced my bare feet to move along the marble tiles lining the floor. As I moved I let my eyes feast on the delicious tableau before me. Jake had his back to the shower door, his head bent at an odd angle as he rinsed shampoo from the left side of his head. Steamy water sluiced over his broad shoulders and made a languid path down his spine, over his lower back, and into the crease of his ass. I had to bite my lip to keep from sighing. Years of training and exercise had honed Jake's body into a work of art. His muscles flexed with every movement. His backside was so round and firm, I thought I could fall on my knees and live out the rest of my life happy to worship it. And though I couldn't see his face right now, a memory of it flashed in my mind. I'd never seen such a perfectly formed face in all my life.

Jake was beautiful.

I came to a halt just outside the shower stall, my hand poised over the door handle. Once I opened the door and stepped inside there was no going back. If I was going to do this I had to commit myself to the venture now. I had to exude confidence, sex appeal, I had to unleash my feminine wiles and--"

"Stella?"

Shit!

"Hi Jake," I said, like the biggest moron ever born.

Jake had turned sometime during my little pep talk to myself. With one hand resting against the shower wall, he regarded me with interest. "Can I help you?"

I opened my mouth, hoping desperately something witty would come out, then deflating when I heard myself saying, "I came to help you."

Dumb! Dumb! Dumb! Help him what?

"Oh?" he wondered, looking sexier than ever.

From behind Jake had been a vision, but head on, chest dripping with steaming water, Jake made my mind go kind of numb. With his hair in glossy black waves and his emerald eyes staring levelly at me, I could barely think. Nevertheless, I motored on. "I thought you could use some help washing your back." *That sounded sort of good.*

"I've already washed my back."

"Your chest then."

"Ditto."

He wasn't making this easy. "I want to do it again," I tried, hoping he wouldn't have anything to say that would counter this.

"Why would you want to do that?"

Think, Stella, think. "Well, you said you wanted me to tell you how much I want you." I paused, glanced up and into his eyes. Shamelessly, I fluttered my lashes. "I'd rather show you."

Though his expression remained grim, I could tell by the way he was looking me up and down that I'd piqued his interest.

"And Dev?"

"He's down in the kitchen," I said, "probably cooking. It's just the two of us."

Jake allowed a sexy, half-smile to flicker over his face, but only for a moment. "Take your clothes off and get in," he said, stepping away from the door.

I slid out of my Jell-O dampened bra and panties so fast I hardly remember doing it. Then I pulled the shower door open and stepped inside. Instantly, the humid air within enveloped me. Water splashed against my shoulders, wetting my hair and bringing me to my senses ... if only for a few seconds.

I couldn't let my hair get wet. What on earth was I thinking? If I did this I was likely to wake with them in the morning looking like a Treasure Troll. And I didn't have any of my hair stuff with me. No frizz serum, no mousse, no hair glosser, no ....

Jake, who seemed to know the way my mind was going, wrapped his arms around my waist and lifted. He set me down a moment later directly beneath the spray of water. Instantly, my hair was saturated, thus making any exodus superfluous.

As I wiped water away from my face with the back of my hand, Jake set one hand on top of the shower stall door and focused on me. "What did you have in mind?"

Being close to this man made my stomach feel so light and airy I wanted to giggle like a middle school girl at an *N SYNC concert. Instead of giggling, though, I reached to my left for the liquid soap. I emptied a handful of the stuff into my palm and rubbed my hands together. Wordlessly, I sank to my knees before him, intending to wash his body from toes to forehead. I was a little caught off guard when Jake crouched with me.

"You think you know what I want?"

I can only suppose that at that moment my expression was a cross between confusion and shock. Nevertheless, I nodded. "You want to be worshipped and adored."

His brow quirked at this. He mumbled something under his breath, then shook his head. "Stand up, Stella. And give me the soap."

"Do what?"

"Stand up and give me the soap."

My mouth fell open. "But I can't," I complained. "That's not what I--" I let the sentence go unfinished, figuring I'd said too much already.

"You're beautiful Stella, but you have a lot to learn about men. Stand up, let me enjoy you."

I thought briefly about being obstinate and refusing, but truth was that I was kind of curious to see what he'd do next. So, with great trepidation, I got to my feet and handed him the soap.

Jake glanced at the bottle and again, shook his head. "Not my soap. I don't want you to smell like me. Grab the Suave. The cucumber and melon that Dev uses. I love the way that smells."

I did as requested, then waited.

Still crouched before me, Jake upended the bottle of Suave, emptied a dollop into his palm, and rubbed. Instantly, the stall was filled with the sweet scent of melons. It was a tropical fragrance, fruity but not so overwhelming it would become annoying.

"Put your foot on my thigh," Jake said, gazing up at me with a slight smile.

This threw me. I'd never seen Jake in such a position before and instantly I wondered what he was up to. "Why?"

"Trust me, Stella." He patted his thigh. "Come on."

I swallowed and lifted my foot. Before I could place it on his thigh, Jake grasped me at the ankle. Gently, he pulled it forward.

"Beautiful feet," he murmured, then did something that boggled my mind. He placed three lingering kisses on my instep.

I may have released a tiny mew of surprise. My head was reeling at this small, loving act. Even as I was searching my mind for possible causes of this sudden gentleness, he began rubbing his lathered hands over my skin.

Goose flesh popped out on my arms and legs and my mind continued to scramble to figure out what was going on. What the hell was Jake doing?

Strong hands stroked my foot, making me shiver. He massaged my toes, stroking me until I thought I'd dissolve into a puddle of steamy water. He ran his thumb over my instep then massaged the delicate flesh with tender caresses. When he'd finished with one foot, he repeated the process with the other. Stroking and rubbing until I was practically purring like a kitten.

His soapy fingers glided up my ankles, over my calves, and along my thighs. He applied just enough pressure to make my muscles loose while rubbing so close to my fevered sex that I nearly cried out every time. His fingers felt like heaven on my skin.

Though he was on his knees, staring intently at me, there was nothing submissive about his posture. His eyes had a look of determination; his lips were set in a succulent O. Although his breathing remained even, his hard cock, jutting up at full attention in his lap, let me know he was very aware of the sensuality of what he was doing.

My stomach felt like a thousand butterflies had taken residence and begun fluttering their wings. The sensation made me feel light and airy. My cunt clenched as mounting need had me panting for release. I wanted Jake, wanted him inside me with a desperation that terrified me.

Showing little sign--save his erection--of the torturous feelings flooding through me, Jake circled my thigh with his hands, running them up and down so close to my cunt I could have cried. He rubbed at my tender skin, stroked, and then used his fingers to massage the last dregs of tension away.

"Please Jake," I said at last. "I can't take anymore."

"You don't want me to bathe you?"

Did I have to draw the man a map. "No. I want … something else."

Jake stood to his full height. "What do you want?" As he spoke he was edging closer. His fingers closed around my waist and he pressed me to the wall.

"Sex! Now!"

That seemed to be what he wanted to hear because a moment later his grip on my waist tightened and he lifted me off the shower floor. "Wrap your legs around my waist. Hold onto my shoulders."

"Yes."

Even as I lifted my legs and drew them around him, he molded his body to mine. His chest, dripping with hot water, grazed my face. He pressed me into the warm tiles and let his hips sink into the circle of my thighs. When our mouths touched, my skin scorched at the point of contact. With a flick of his tongue, he prodded my lips, bidding me to open for him. I realized then that Jake wasn't as calm as he'd been pretending to be. He speared my lips and delved within, feasting on my mouth with a hunger that incited an inferno in me.

I squirmed in his arms, delighting in his male flavor even as I welcomed him within, greedy for more. My hands moved along his shoulders and down his back as he deepened the kiss. I couldn't get enough of him.

We ravished each other, let the kiss go on until we were both so desperate for sex, we couldn't think of anything else.

Jake drew back and caught his breath. "Tell me you want me, Stella."

"I want you, Jake."

His grip on my waist tightened as he flexed his hips. The pressure of his cock against my opening made my head swim. I swallowed down a sigh and licked my lips as a wave of hot lust descended on me.

He flexed his hips again, tested my readiness. When he found me dripping wet, he bit his lower lip and thrust up.

The impression of being filled flooded my body. My inner channel vibrated with the sweetest of sensations. I scored his back with my nails and cried out.

Jake gasped, seemed surprised at the intensity of this coupling. Then he gazed at me and gritted his teeth. "Hold on. It's too much. I can't be gentle with you. Is that all right?"

I clenched my thighs in response. "I don't want you to be gentle."

With a growl of pure male need, Jake twined his fingers in my hair and jerked my head back. His lips and teeth were on my throat, then he began to move and there was nothing but the thrill of being thoroughly ridden.

With one arm locked around my waist, the other twined in my hair, Jake drove into me hard and fast, setting off a multitude of luscious vibrations in my body. Pleasure filled my womb.

"This is so good," Jake said against my throat.

My arms fastened around his neck and held firm.

In quick succession he plunged into me then withdrew, plunged deep, then withdrew. His hips had the fevered rhythm of a well-oiled piston. Too soon I felt tightness in my stomach. The lush tickling of my womb grew more intense until I felt I'd explode if I couldn't release the tension.

"Slower, Jake. I'm so close. Too close."

"I. Can't. Stop," he said, speaking a word with every thrust.

I knew water was running over my face and down our bodies. Knowing the end was near, feeling my climax hovering just out of reach, I reared up and found Jake's lips.

Hungrily we kissed. He devoured my mouth even as I gorged myself on him. I sucked his tongue into my depths and let my own dance against it. Panting as my release drew nearer, on the verge of tears, I moaned into his mouth.

Overcome by his own emotions, Jake began pumping faster, driving into me so hard my toes curled. I knew then that I'd reached the end of my tether. I couldn't hold on any longer. "Can I cum?" I asked Jake, mindless of the desperation in my voice.

In answer, his eyes rolled into his head. He managed to ground out a single word, "Yes," before his orgasm drove him completely over the edge.

The tightening in my belly gave way. I threw my head back, screaming out my release and my climax descended on me.

I bucked in Jake's steel grip, twisted in an erotic dance of euphoria. The pleasure came at me in stages, each more intense and powerful than the last. I couldn't stop whimpering, couldn't stop crying Jake's name.

When I finally felt myself returning to earth, exhausted and completely spent, I let my head flop against Jake's shoulder. "Stick a fork in me--I'm done."

* * * *

I woke sometime in the middle of the night to the sound of quiet voices. I rolled onto my back and stared up at the ceiling. The room was dark, save the glow of the flames in the fireplace. A quick glance at the bed showed me I was alone. Put two and two together and I figured the phantom voices belonged to Jake and Dev. But what were they doing?

Moving slowly, so as not to make any noise, I rolled onto my right hip and arched up until I caught sight of them.

I nearly moaned.

Jake and Dev were sprawled on the rug in front of the fireplace, absolutely naked. Though I could have been mistaken--but I highly doubted it--they looked poised for action. Sex Action, as the eighties rock band, LA Guns, would have said.

Sounding breathless and eager, Jake spoke to Dev in a raspy voice that made gooseflesh pop out along my skin. "Get on your stomach, Dev."

Dev was on his backside, his cock standing at full attention between his spread legs. He smirked at Jake. "I think I'd rather fuck you tonight."

I was right! They were about to have sex. I'd never seen them have sex without me between them. Never! I should have had a few reservations about the proceedings; after all, seeing the two of them entwined without me was bound to make me jealous. But the only emotion I felt was anticipation.

"You woke me up, remember," Jake said, still speaking in a hush. "Asked me to fuck you, remember? You said you wanted a rough quickie."

"Maybe I changed my mind."

Jake chuckled. "I don't think so. I think you let yourself get turned on while you were watching Stella and me in the Jell-O. I think you got so turned on you haven't been able to think about anything all night except getting fucked."

"Maybe I'd like to have you flat on your stomach tonight getting an ass full of *my* dick."

"That's not gonna happen." Jake climbed to his feet and stood with his legs wide and his hands settled on his hips.

Dev took one look at Jake and grinned. "On second thought, why don't you make me?"

Dev had barely finished the sentence when Jake sprang forward.

The force of having all of Jake's body hurled at him so unexpectedly at him seemed to have caught Dev off guard. Jake fell on Dev, pinning Dev's more lithe body to the floor beneath his solid one. Using Dev's surprise to his advantage, Jake hoisted himself up long enough to flip Dev onto his stomach.

Dev landed with a grunt but still managed to get his arms under himself faster than I would have. I saw his muscles tense as his body readied for action.

"I'm so gonna kick your ass when I get up, Jake," Dev promised. The threat would have been more convincing if he wasn't laughing while he said it.

He'd begun to push up but Jake threw himself on top of Dev. Once again, the surprise of having to carry all of Jake's weight was enough to drive Dev into the floor.

Taking advantage of his dominant position, Jake straddled Dev's ass then caught his wrists. Though it seemed to take all of Jake's strength, he managed to force Dev's arms down and pin them to the floor.

"You're not gonna do anything, are you?" Jake taunted.

Dev bared his teeth. Again, his muscles tensed as he readied himself for another go at flipping over. But before he could do anything, Jake slid his cock between Dev's ass cheeks and slid inside.

Damn! I hoped Jake had been lubed up before he'd done that. Otherwise, ouch.

The determined grimace Dev had been wearing dissolved into one of total and complete pleasure. His eyes rolled into the back of his head and he moaned.

I nearly sat bolt upright so I could watch the unfolding scene with ease. It was like having my very own erotic male triple X movie happening in front of me. All I needed was soda and popcorn.

Jake's eyes whipped to me. "Go into the bedside table and get me the handcuffs."

I did sit bolt upright then. "Huh? I didn't see a thing."

When I stared dumbly at him, he pointed at the drawer. "Get the handcuffs."

Without thinking about the ramifications of what I was doing (like the fact that Dev was likely to retaliate somehow once Jake set him loose), I crawled to the aforementioned bedside table, pulled the drawer out and fished around till my anxious little fingers closed around the cuffs. "Here you go." I crawled to the edge of the bed and placed them in Jake's waiting hand.

"Thank you, Stella. Now go back to bed." He spoke quietly, but firmly, so I knew he'd meant it.

I settled back in the bed and pulled the covers to my throat, staring unabashedly at them the entire time. It only took me a few seconds to prop the pillows under my head so I could spy on the unfolding scene and be comfortable at the same time.

Shameful, I know, but who could blame me?

I wondered briefly why Jake thought he needed the handcuffs. Dev had stopped fighting him once he had slid inside.

I nearly cried out when Jake tightened his hold on Dev's arm and jerked it unceremoniously into a cuff. Was this the man who was always schooling Dev on being gentle with me? Damn, if he tried that with me he would have broken my arm.

"Are you trying to break my arm?" Dev inquired quietly.

"You know you like it rough." He set Dev's other arm in a cuff. The click of the metal locking into place filled the quiet room. "That's better, isn't it?" Jake flexed his thighs as he spoke and plunged deep.

Dev groaned. "Shit, Jake, just fuck me."

And he did.

As I watched, like the voyeur I was, Jake began to thrust in and out of Dev. His movements were deliberately slow at first; each penetration designed to pull a desperate moan out of Dev. But as Dev's moans became more intense, Jake increased his pace, driving into Dev hard and fast.

"You belong to me, Dev," Jake said through gritted teeth as he rode Dev harder. "You and Stella are mine."

When Dev didn't answer, Jake bent forward and eased his hand under Dev's hip. The moment it closed around Dev's cock Dev began to pant. "Yeah, just like that, Jake."

"You like that?"

"Oh yeah."

Watching them together, seeing the pinkish flush on their skin and the glistening sheen of perspiration on their bodies made me realize anew just how beautiful they both were. Two strong and healthy male bodies entwined in pleasure. I suddenly grasped the fact that the two strong and healthy male bodies belonged to me just as much as they belonged to each other. I was glad they'd allowed me to see this. I thought that maybe this meant we were truly more than sex buddies. That we were lovers.

Dev gasped for breath and pushed back against Jake. "Fuck, I'm gonna cum."

Jake fell lengthwise over Dev and milked the orgasm out of him.

They moved together, thrusting and groaning, until Jake collapsed on top of Dev and Dev released into Jake's palm.

I lay quietly for a few seconds, waiting for one of them to move. But after a full minute passed without either of them uttering so much as a sound I realized they'd fallen asleep.

I went to the linen closet down the hall from the bedroom and extracted a clean, white sheet from within. After I covered them, just in case they got cold, I climbed back into bed and fell into a deep, restful sleep.

Chapter Thirteen

Journal Entry 3/28/05, 4:22 PM

Hmmm.
Stella Marie Rice-Santos!
Stella Marie Rice-Chambers!
Stella Rice-Santos … Stella Rice-Chambers?
Stella Santos Chambers?
Argh!

* * * *

5:02 PM

Disaster! Disaster!
Dear God, I've finally done it. I've finally done it and I
sure as shit don't like it. I said those three little words that
no self-respecting woman ever says to a man unless she's
sure the guy feels the same. *Argh!*
What was I thinking? It just sort of slipped out before I
could stop it.
Stupid, stupid, stupid Stella!
I'm so embarrassed.
I'm never leaving my house aga … *Argh!* I'm not in my
house, I'm in their house. The moment I go downstairs,
chances are I'll come across them again.
This is the most horrid day of my life.

* * * *

5:14 PM

Feel much calmer now. Have had a few minutes to sit
back and reflect on the catastrophe and put things into
perspective. Probably things aren't as bad as I fear.
Probably I'm making more of this than needs be. Probably
they didn't even believe me.
It all started out simple enough. I went down to the
kitchen while Dev was making dinner. The scent of fresh
salmon and steaming broccoli filled my nostrils as soon as I
came within twenty feet of the kitchen. Sighing with

pleasure as my stomach gave a rumble of hunger, I checked that the bodice of my sundress was displaying just enough cleavage to have another part of Dev's body rumbling with sexual hunger. The baby blue dress had a hemline that fell just below my thighs, making it short enough to show off my legs while maintaining enough modesty so as not to make me look too obvious.

Barefoot, hungry, and surprisingly horny, I sauntered into the kitchen.

Dev was settled at the table, a mug of fragrant coffee to the left of him and a legal sized pad full of Dev's tiny scribbling to the right. I sashayed by the table, careful to work my hips as I went. At the stove I peaked into the oven and made a point of moaning and groaning my appreciation.

"Smells fantastic!" I announced, a little too brightly.

"No picking at it."

I walked to the table and settled across from him. "I can wait till dinner."

"I don't have ask if you enjoyed yourself last night."

My face grew hot, and not for the first time I thanked the stars above that my skin didn't show when I was embarrassed.

One perfectly coiffed eyebrow arched and Dev raised his head from the pad. "Think you'll be up to taking the both of us soon?"

I sensed challenge in the air, so I deftly changed the subject. "Whatcha writing?"

Grinning, he sat back in his chair and met my gaze. His chocolate eyes fixed on mine and held steady. Even as he lifted the mug of coffee to his mouth and swallowed, he continued to stare at me. A tiny chirp of pleasure seeped from me. My heart kicked up a beat and I sucked in a breath.

He'd come down to breakfast wearing a pair of tattered jeans and nothing else. His nipples were pink as the inside of a freshly shored seashell. The peaks hardened as I gazed at him, the tender flesh around it puckering.

Seeing the path my eyes were on, Dev crossed his arms over his chest. The move set off a ripple of muscular activity in his biceps, what it didn't do was shield the pebbly peaks of his nipples.

Still smiling, he observed, "You look hungry, Stella."

"Maybe I am."

Licking his lips, he placed his thumb and forefinger around the turgid peak and squeezed. "Want a taste of me?"

I whimpered.

"I bet you want more than a taste," he said, continuing to draw my attention to his lush body by pinching the purpling flesh. "I bet you'd love it if I came around the table, spread your thighs, and ... well ... you know."

"Right here?"

He released his nipple and sat back. "I'm working on lyrics."

"Huh?"

"Lyrics. You asked what I was writing."

My eyes danced from his pursed lips to his nipples, then over the rigid lines of his chest. "Oh yeah. I did, didn't I? Well, I think we should talk some more about this tasting thing."

"Oh yeah?"

"Yeah."

He pushed away from the table, stood, and crossed to the oven, speaking over his shoulder as he pulled the tray of salmon from within. "Keep it up, Stella, and I'll think you only like me for by body."

"It's the only reason I let you hang around." Wearing a pair of worn-in Levis, Jake strutted into the kitchen and joined Dev at the stove. "How's that ass, Dev?"

Dev rolled my eyes. "A little sore, but I'll live, but thanks for asking. Next time using a little more lube won't hurt you. And stop picking at my food. I hate it when you do that. Wait till I get it on the table."

Jake mumbled something profane, and then popped the stolen chunk of meat into his mouth. "I am so hungry I feel like I'll die if I don't get something to eat soon." As he spoke, he was sidling closer to the meat.

"Stay back. You'll ruin it if you keep picking at it."

"It's gonna end up in our stomach's anyway. What's the big deal?"

Silent, I watched them. Even as I stood there, heart welling with all sorts of girly emotions, I knew I should run. Instinct told me if I didn't leave the room and get some fresh air to clear my head I was likely to do something stupid.

But I didn't *do* anything stupid. I watched Dev cut the salmon and place the sections on three dishes while Jake began piling broccoli in artless heaps beside the meat, setting Dev off. I didn't do anything, but I didn't have to. Opening my mouth was enough.

"Shit! I think I'm falling in love with you. With both of you."

The room went quiet. Jake turned slowly, faced me … and smiled.

Dev glanced at me, winked, and then he and Jake exchanged a look. I'd elaborate on that look if I could, but I can't. It was a look.

Jake's smile broadened. "Of course you are."

"Maybe that's why she always so horny."

Then we ate dinner. I tell them I'm falling in love and they serve me food. I'm completely and utterly humiliated.

Chapter Fourteen

Journal Entry 3/29/05, 8:42 PM

I sat on a fat pillow, my legs curled beneath me and my skirt spread out against my thighs. A fire was roaring in the fireplace positioned a foot from the table's edge, filling our little Shangri la with warm light. A series of ornately decorated wall recesses held flickering candles whose soft light made our Mediterranean surroundings seem even more lush and vibrant than usual. It was romance at its best, luxury at it's most opulent, and I was with my three best friends.

"I think you should cut your losses and move on," Katarina was advising me between delicate sips of her apple martini. "If they didn't reciprocate, the relationship is doomed."

I sighed. Seemed I'd been sighing all night. "But Dev sort of told me he loved me the other day at my place." I paused to look each of my friends in the eye. "And I think he meant it."

Ann, who'd been surveying her bottle of MGD with doubt, abruptly looked at me over the mouth of her beer. A slight crease formed between her eyes as she frowned. "Were you serious when you said it?"

I shrugged. "I don't know."

"I think you do."

"I don't know," I insisted. "All I'm saying is Jake and Dev are special. They're good men."

Meagan arched an eyebrow. "Tell me you were just emotional; tell me you're not really falling in love with them."

Katarina cried out. "No Stella! Say you're not."

Ann continued to study me over her beer.

I shrugged, sighed, and then shrugged again. Silently I ran the name, Stella Marie Santos-Chambers over my tongue a few times to see how it felt. Stella Santos-Chambers had a better ring. It was short, sweet, and simple.

"Stella!"

I blinked, and then realized I was the focus of intense scrutiny.

"Stella, no," Katarina continued. "Take that dopey look off your face. You're not in love with them. Say it with me one time, come on and say it. I don't love Devlin Chambers and I don't love--" she stopped when she realized she was the only one speaking.

Meagan eyed me. "Damn it, Stella. Are you kidding me? You're setting yourself up to get hurt."

"It sure as shit looks like she's in love with them," Ann answered for me.

"Don't be silly. I'm not in love with Dev or Jake or anyone else. All I was saying is that I could grow to love them. They're both special to me and I'm going to do whatever I can to make sure things work out between us."

"Because you can't have a serious relationship with two bisexual men, you realize." Meagan lifted her oversized margarita glass to her lips and took a sip. "They have a penchant for men. It's something that'll always be there."

Liking the direction of Meagan's advice, Katarina jumped in. "She's right."

Dev and Stella Chambers? Stella and Jake Santos?

"Are you listening to us?"

"Huh? Of course I'm listening. But this conversation is irrelevant." At least I was trying to. I started off listening, but somehow my thoughts veered away from the conversation. I began to wonder if Dev was home or not, and if he was what he was doing? Was he having sex with Jake? Was Jake naked and laying with Dev this very minute, maybe thinking about me? Were they wishing I was there between them as I'd been so many times before? The thrill of being sandwiched between two gorgeous men, of knowing I was the object of their desire.

"Stella!"

Chapter Fifteen

Journal Entry 4/5/05, 7:52 AM

I lay in my bed, phone affixed to the side of my head, trying desperately not to scream at the top of my lungs.

Mother: I just don't understand it Stella. You're a beautiful girl, yet you seem bound and determined to be a spinster all of your life.

Me: I'm not a spinster, mommy. I happen to be happy with my life the way it is.

Mother: I find that hard to believe.

Me: Be that as it may, I am happy. I have a fulfilling career, great friends--"

Mother: And some white man with too much hair that's at your house till all hours of the night.

Is this my life? I mean, is this really my life?

Me: *Silence.*

Mother: That's right. Sadie told me. Said you were standing outside your apartment ... *outside* your apartment kissing! Kissing! Now I know I raised my girls better than that."

Me: *Silence.*

Mother: Stella Marie Rice, are you listening to me?

Me: I'm not discussing my personal life with you. It's my business.

Mother: And you're my business.

Me: I have to go.

Mother: Tell me the truth, Stella. Is my baby girl fornicating with a WASP? With a White-Anglo-Saxon--

Me: I love you, mom. Talk to you soon.

I disconnected.

WASP? Had my mother really just called Dev a WASP? There was no way in the world I could bring him to my mother's house. But now that she knew about him, I couldn't see any way I couldn't.

* * * *

Journal Entry 4/7/05, 4:49 PM

Lately it seemed everybody wanted to buy me a dress. I didn't mind it so much when it was Dev on the other end of the credit card, but when it was my mom wielding the plastic I wasn't so thrilled.

Me and the aforementioned parent were in Columbia, Maryland, in Nordstrom Café in the Columbia Mall. We'd been there since a little after one, shopping for a birthday dress. It was like I was turning sixteen all over again, but really, what could I do? It was my mom! She'd given me life, fed me, reared me, saw to my education, paid for my first two years of college. If she wanted to buy me a birthday dress I couldn't say no, even if this whole thing was a transparent scheme to get me alone and so she could drill me about my love life.

"Devlin Chambers," she muttered, sipping her tea. "I suppose that sounds respectable enough. How old did you say he was?"

I hadn't said. "Twenty-seven."

She carefully set her mug on the gleaming table and stared at me. Her thin lips drew down into a frown just as one eyebrow rose into a high, aristocratic arch. "Come again?"

"Twenty-seven." I beamed, hoping that a smile would minimize the fact that Dev was younger than me.

"And he's a--" she reached for her teacup yet again and took two bracing swallows. Was there Jack in that cup or what? She was on her fifth already. Hell, she'd been going at the stuff like it was laced with gold. "He's a musician. Is that right?"

Why couldn't Sadie have walked in on me making out with Jake, why couldn't I be discussing Jake with my mother right now? Sure, Jake wasn't black, but he was half Puerto Rican and Native American, to someone like my mother that was the next best thing. On top of Jake's minority status, he owned a popular gym in Baltimore, a condo on the harbor, Jake was so much better on paper than Dev. "He's brilliant, mom. He has an amazing range. And he looks absolutely fantastic in leather."

"I'm sure he does. Be that as it may, I really don't think he's the kind of man you could have a future with. I think you'd fit better with someone like Steven."

'Mom, Steven and I were over a long time ago. That was high school, I was sixteen. I'm almost thirty-one now."

"And dating a man four years younger than you, I mean really, Stella. What kind of life can this Devlin character offer you? What kind of money does he make?"

I fingered the handle on my cup, debated taking a sip from my own tepid tea. When we'd ordered I'd had a craving for green tea, but that craving had passed, along with my appetite. "He does okay."

"And what does he plan to do when he's not so young anymore and doesn't look so cute prancing around the stage in leather? Does he have a musical degree?"

"I don't know."

"Don't you think you should find out? I mean really, Stella, how will he support you?"

"I don't need a man to support me. I support myself just fine. And I'm not with Dev because of money. I'm with him because I care deeply about him. I think I may actually be falling in love with him."

My mother froze, mouth agape. For a good five seconds she didn't move, then, before I could react, she proceeded to drop her nearly full cup tea. It seemed to descend in slow motion, somersaulting through the air and sending hot Earl Grey flying in every direction. I saw a brief flash of myself leaping across the table and catching the cup before it made impact, but knew I'd never be fast enough.

The teacup hit the floor with a sharp *crash*. Fine bits of porcelain jettisoned into the air like tiny projectiles.

Like a veteran actress who knows her part well, my mother promptly clutched her throat and began to choke. What she could be choking on, I had no idea. She hadn't been drinking before she'd let the cup fall and there wasn't any food anywhere on our table.

For a few seconds I stared at my splattered white blouse, annoyed that I'd have to pay to have it dry cleaned again when I'd just gotten it back from the dry cleaner on Monday. Then, as various worried strangers began to inundate the table, I realized that perhaps I should do something about my mother. "Are you all right, mommy?"

Eyes narrowed to thin slits, she regarded me over the table me with displeasure. She must have realized I wasn't impressed with the choking bit. Not even a little bit.

Unfortunately for her she'd already begun the whole choking performance. Now that she had the attention of everyone within a million mile radius she had to play it out.

Okay, I know I might sound harsh, but I'd seen my mother's theatrics before. This was her M.O. She'd learned early on in life that there was nothing better than mortality to keep people in check, especially her kids. It used to work like a charm, but when I'd hit twenty-five and saw she was still alive and kicking, the effect had dulled.

"I'm all right," she was saying to an older man a few minutes later. This guy had taken a particular interest in my mother, sticking around even after the mess was cleaned up and everyone else had returned to their tables. "Like I said, the tea must have gone down the wrong way."

"I told you that you were drinking too fast," I offered, helpfully.

Eyes rimmed with faux tears, my mother went for her purse and excavated her wallet from within. "Well, this was nice Stella Marie. But I have to get you home. I have to get in touch with Reese and make sure things are running smoothly in the food department, the florist says--"

"The florist? Come on, mom, do we really need a florist? The house is perfect as is."

She blinked. "Don't be ridiculous, Stella. I won't have that Devlin character coming into our home and looking down on us."

I wanted to roll my eyes, but managed to restrain myself. "Dev's not like that. He's excited to meet you. Besides, there's nothing wrong with our house."

She pulled a few bills from her wallet and tossed them on the table. "Apparently there is. Why else haven't you brought that Devlin boy over?"

I couldn't win. I simply could not win. "You'll meet him soon enough." I followed her to the exit, careful not to show how annoyed I was.

We left the mall and crossed to her car in silence. It wasn't until we were in the car and heading east on Little Patuxent Parkway that she began speaking again.

"We didn't find an appropriate dress today, but that's all right. I'll come get you tomorrow afternoon and we'll go to Arundel Mills."

I tried not to squirm in my seat. "I'm not going to be able to shop tomorrow."

The temperature in the car seemed to drop a good twenty degrees. "Why not?"

"I've sort of got plans."

"What sort of plans? Don't tell me you're refusing to see me in favor of that Devlin person."

"He's taking me to a masquerade ball. We've been planning to go for weeks now. I can't cancel. I don't want to cancel." I added.

She was quiet.

We merged onto I95 and I stared miserably out the window. Shopping with my mom had been a complete disaster. Not only was my birthday dinner destined to be a catastrophe, but I was pulling Dev into it. And what should I do about Jake? How could I explain to him that I was bringing Dev to my house but not him?

It was all one big mess.

"Go to your little ball, then," my mother said. "I'll find a dress for you."

I was too exhausted to argue. I gave her a weak smile, nodded, and then turned the radio on.

My birthday dinner will be my most humiliating day ever. I just know it.

Chapter Sixteen

Journal Entry 4/8/05, 8:49 PM

I gazed at my reflection in the mirror and grimaced. "You've got to be kidding me." I shifted to the right, then the left. It didn't help.

I was in the master bathroom of Jake and Dev's place, trying very hard to figure out what in the hell I was doing. I looked like a moron. The dress--if you could call it a dress--was short and see-through, as in, very short and very see-through. If I didn't know better I'd think Jake and Dev had gone to the grocery store and picked up some red Saran Wrap and sown it into the general shape of a dress. This was crazy! I wasn't going out in public like this.

Though I'd slithered into the dress with relative ease, it fit like a second skin. Sleeveless, strapless, and tasteless, I looked like I was wearing a large, plastic, tube top. I gazed at my reflection again and I could see the brown peaks of my nipples showing through, as well as the red Victoria's Secret thong I'd put on this evening.

I set my hands on my hips and spun toward the door. "No way! You guys hear me, no way!" I knew they were on the other side of the door, waiting, but they could wait till hell froze over. I was not going out in public looking like a tarted up lollipop. "No way!"

The knob jangled. The muffled sound of male voices slithered within, then Jake was pushing the door open. I took a step back and readied myself for verbal war. Unfortunately, the moment I caught a look at Jake my mind went loopy.

He'd taken a page from GQ and gone with a very swanky tuxedo. Black slacks, immaculate white shirt, and a black jacket that made him look like a Hollywood heartthrob. His jacket hung open and I could see his wine pink nipples through his gauzy shirt as he stepped through the entrance and into the room.

He came into the room far enough for Dev to step into the doorway, then Jake leaned against the wall and eyed me from my bare feet to the top of my head.

While Jake decided whether or not I was up to par, Dev nodded his approval. "Lovely. You look wonderful, kitten. Good enough to eat."

I wanted to say "Ha!" and tell him to go bonk himself. Instead, I took in the black slacks, lined with thin burgundy pinstripes, pinstripe jacket, and ruffled burgundy shirt and giggled. Upon his head he'd set a black top hat.

"Very nice, Stella," Jake decided. "You fill that dress perfectly. I had feared you'd be too thin."

Too thin my ass. Since I'd met Jake I had gained five pounds.

Jake pushed off from the wall and offered me his arm. "Are we ready then?"

A million responses filtered through my mind. That the dress looked stupid, that I wouldn't be caught dead in such a monstrosity, that red wasn't my color. You can imagine my surprise when I saw myself entangle my arm with his. No doubt I was smiling like a buffoon.

He led me forward and toward the door. "There are a few ground rules."

With great effort I suppressed the groan that nearly bubbled out. "What sort of ground rules?"

Jake led me to the bed where two pink boxes rested on the coverlet. He began ticking points off on his fingers while Dev lifted a box and began toying with it. It was hard concentrating on what Jake was saying, having my full focus on the boxes as it was. I wondered if they'd gotten me presents. A pretty little surprise from each man.

I smiled happily at the thought.

"Stella?" Jake nudged my chin with a finger. "Are you listening to me?"

"Huh? Oh, yeah. Of course."

"You don't speak unless Dev or I ask you a direct question or give you permission to speak."

That got my attention. "What!"

"We'll only be asking you yes or no questions, so you won't be saying much in any case."

"Wait a minute, back up. I'm not supposed to talk unless you say I can? Bullshit!" If the look of total shock on

Jake's face was anything to go by you'd think speech was a newly acquired skill and one I wasn't entirely comfortable using. How dare he tell me I wasn't allowed to speak. "How dare you!"

Dev continued to fiddle with the box, turning it this way and that but making no real attempt to open it. "We're taking you to a masquerade ball. A fetish masquerade ball, kitten. No sub is allowed to--"

"Sub? I'm going to a fetish ball as a submissive?"

Dev grinned. "I told you she'd refuse if we'd told her ahead of time."

Jake nodded sagely. "It's not a big deal. They'll be lots of subs there. You won't be the only one. And you're going to have a good time. Have I steered you wrong yet?"

He had a point there, but I wasn't ready to cede it. "What other rules would I have to follow?"

Jake stared at me for a moment. His green eyes moved over my face so intently my skin began to crawl. "You will refer to Dev as Lord and me as Master."

My mouth fell open. He had to be kidding. "My Lord and Master? Bullshit!"

Clearly warming to his theme, Jake continued. "If Dev asks you a question your appropriate response is either yes My Lord, or no My Lord."

I wanted to kick him.

"Your eyes are to remain on me or Dev at all times. They'll be plenty of attractive men there, Stella, and I'm a very jealous man. If I find you staring at any male save Dev or me I won't be pleased."

He took my silence for ascent. "Very good. Last is the matter of your collar."

That did it. That just completely did it. I slammed my fists against my hips and glared at him. "Have you lost your ever loving mind? I am not wearing a collar."

Jake thrust his fists against his hips. His eyes thinned to slits. "If you're going with us, you are. I refuse to fight off every man who sees you and decides he'd like to have you."

"Well maybe I'm not going with you."

His lip curled. "Is that right?"

"Damn skippy."

Jake's lips spread wide as he prepared to say something that would no doubt be stupider than anything he'd said thus far, but at that precise moment, Dev stepped in. "Why don't you warm the car up and pull it around front? We'll be down in a few minutes."

Jake looked mutinous.

I raised my brow and met his glare head on.

"We can't knock her out and drag her with us against her will," Dev continued, rather sensibly I thought. He settled his palm on Jake's shoulder and gave Jake a gentle prod toward the door. "See you in a few minutes."

Jake allowed himself to be moved. Slowly, head still bent toward me, he took another step toward the door. "If you try to duck out of this Stella, I won't be happy."

I tossed my hair over a shoulder and shrugged. "Oh big whoop, what's new?"

Jake began to turn back.

"Get out already." Dev waved toward the door. "You're not helping."

With a sort of growling sound, Jake marched to the door then disappeared into the hall. Once he was gone, Dev went to the bedside table where a nearly empty bottle of Pinot Grigio was sitting. They'd been plying me with wine since I'd gotten there, and I could see why now.

He poured a fresh glass and brought it to the bed where he settled himself. "Come sit?" He patted the comforter. His large, bejeweled fingers were oddly enticing. I had a brief flash of the things he'd done to me with those fingers, a memory of how good they could make me feel.

Face hot with embarrassment over my thoughts, I obliged. I had to clear my throat a few times before speech was possible. "My friends are right. Jake has some serious control issues. The nerve of him to assume--" Dev held the wine glass out to me but I shook my head. "I've had enough wine already."

He shrugged, then drank from the glass himself. "You're right about Jake. He does like being in control. It's that gorgeous face of his. It simply doesn't occur to him that anyone would want to do anything other than what he tells them to do."

"Even you?"

He set the empty wineglass on the bedside table then licked his lips. His pink tongue moved languidly over the succulent flesh, so slowly I was momentarily transfixed. I could feel my heart rate go double time as I watched him. Something in the pit of my belly began to awaken and swirl about.

"I'm different. I like to be in control too so he knows not to push me too far. We butt heads otherwise."

I forced my eyes away from him and tried to focus on something far less enticing ... the comforter. Unfortunately my eyes persisted in sneaking quick little glances at him. I took in his handsome face and the broad expanse of his chest where, despite his shirt, I could see an outline of muscle. His velvet sheathed thighs were muscle laden as well, and I was having a damn hard time keeping my hands folded in my lap instead of scurrying all over his. The man was too sexy for his own good.

Endeavoring for a calm voice, I informed Dev that, "I'm not wearing a collar."

Dev reclined on one elbow and studied me. "The collar is non-negotiable. A collar signifies to trolling Doms that you are taken and accounted for and not on the market. Jake was right. If you don't wear a collar we'll be staving off the attention of Dominants--male and female I might add--all night." He lifted one of the pink boxes onto his lap and pulled the top off. "We had this made for you last month." He pulled a red leather collar from within.

It was a pretty thing, as far collars went, but I didn't know if that was the norm. They'd had faux diamonds etched into the leather into the pattern of a rose on either side of the metal hook where the lead was to be attached. The collar was about three inches wide so I figured it wouldn't be uncomfortable were I to wear it. "I don't know, Dev. What if someone there knows me and sees me wearing a collar?"

"First off, what would they be doing there in the first place if they were the sort to judge you? Secondly, it's a masquerade party. Everyone will be wearing a mask. It's pretend. You shouldn't take it so seriously."

"And if it were you who had to wear the collar?"

"I have worn a collar. So has Jake as a matter of fact, but he hated every second. He was even more overbearing and controlling in a collar than he was out of it ... if you can imagine that." He laughed quietly and I figured he was remembering Jake frothing at the mouth.

"I don't think I'd want to put Jake in a collar."

"I can be a very ruthless master so I didn't have a problem handling him. But my point is we've all done the collar bit. It's all in fun." He nudged my chin up with one of those perfectly formed fingers. The one wearing the exquisite ruby. His chocolate gaze was unwavering as he slid the red collar beneath my hair and wrapped it around my neck. Hot breath peppered my face as he breathed, opened-mouthed, against my cheek.

"You're not really our slave." He tightened the first buckle, slid his tongue over his lower lip. "We don't really own you. We just get off on pretending we do." He pulled the second buckle tight and slid it into place, sort of contradicting his words. "And I think if you were honest with yourself you'd admit that you get off on it, too. Don't you?"

Carnal need had enveloped me so thoroughly I didn't trust myself to speak. I wanted Dev to lay me down, collar and all, and take me there and then. I was desperate to have him pinion my body beneath his, eager for him to impale me.

"Don't you?"

I swallowed. "Maybe just a little bit."

"I think it's more than a little bit." He settled a hand on my bare knee and I jumped. "I think you love the idea of giving me and Jake total control. I think there's nothing in the world you'd love to do more than go to that party with me and Jake, wearing our collar. I think you love the idea of every person who sees you knowing who you belong to." He squeezed my knee and slid closer. "Isn't that right, kitten?"

A strong cocktail of lust and humiliation was confusing my thoughts. He was right, but the fact that I was so transparent was mortifying.

"It's nothing to be embarrassed of. We're adults, we enjoy sex, we enjoy fantasy. That's normal. Fear of one's carnal desires. That's not normal."

He had a point. But I was still embarrassed. What modern woman was aroused by the idea of being led around on a leash by two men? It simply wasn't done in the twenty-first century.

I moaned when he brushed his lips over mine. When he spoke, his voice was gruff with what I guessed was desire. "I'll make you a promise."

"What's that?"

He gave my upper lip a nibble, then a lick, and I nearly passed out. "You come with us to this party and play by our rules and if after thirty minutes you're not enjoying yourself or you're uncomfortable, we'll go home."

"Jake?"

"Jake will agree. He won't make you do anything you're uncomfortable with."

The nibbles deepened. His mouth closed over mine and he delved in for a taste. I closed my eyes and would have fallen onto my back had he not wrapped his arms around me. His lips were soft yet demanding and he tasted of wine. I reveled in his taste and breathed him in.

Too soon he drew away. There was a bit of red lip gloss on him now, but I was too aroused to point it out.

"What do you say, kitten? Have we got ourselves a deal?"

I'd go anywhere with this man. "Yes."

"Wonderful." He stood. "You're going to have a great time. And when you're caught up in the party and thinking things can't get any better, I'm gonna take you someplace completely private and fuck you senseless."

I stared up and into his dark gaze, so turned on that all thoughts of my collar, my dress, and my "ownership" were forgotten. "Is that a promise?"

He cupped the bulge in his pants and grinned. "What do you think?"

* * * *

9:17 PM

We arrived at our destination much sooner than I'd anticipated. I was nervous and felt like a complete moron in my glossy red dress and spiky heels. Situated in the Jag on Dev's lap, I was surrounded by a wonderfully warm body and wasn't prepared to get out of the car to walk to the front door in the cold. I was with Jake and Dev, precisely where I wanted to be. I didn't need a party to have a good time.

From the driver's seat and to my left, Jake looped the lead of my collar around his fist and gave it a gentle tug.

Immediately my head dipped forward. Much as I would have preferred it to be otherwise, that small movement had my already fevered body giddy with need. "Still remember the rules?"

I would have nodded had Jake not had such a thorough hold of the chain. "Yes. You're yes master and Dev is yes lord. I don't speak unless spoken to and I don't stare at other men."

"And you keep your eyes on us."

Dev gave my thigh a squeeze. "Are you nervous, kitten?"

"A bit."

"You'll enjoy yourself. I promise." As he spoke, he took off his hat then slid on his mask. It was basic black, rather plain, but once it was on it gave him the roguish good looks of Zorro. Jake had a mask that was an exact match to Dev's, and I had no doubt that he'd look just as sexy in his.

Dev nodded, indicating the red mask in my lap. Mine was more elaborate than theirs. It was made of crushed velvet and had creamy white swirls of pearl and crystal etched into it in an ornate pattern of doves in flight. I slipped the mask over my head and into place then tried to smile.

I felt ridiculous.

"Look, we're here." Dev motioned out of the windshield toward what I could only suppose was a house. It could have been a private hospital, five-star hotel, or the home of some Hollywood starlet. The sight of the looming structure did nothing to quell my fear. Rather, it made my unease about a thousand times worse.

The house was situated on an ordinary suburban street. Tall pines and old oaks lined the road. A sidewalk ran along the street before the pretty, two-story houses opposite our destination. Though the night was dark, I spied a hopscotch grid drawn in red chalk beneath an iron streetlamp. Lawns were perfectly manicured and houses were well cared for. It was all very quaint and picturesque until you saw the forbidding gray structure whose property took up a full two blocks of real estate. The house was much larger than its neighbors. It stood on a grassy knoll surrounded by massive pines and weeping willows. The house itself seemed a modern stereotype of the gothic architectural style. It was made of gray stone that was partially hidden beneath patches of ivy. Two turrets stood like four-story bookends on either side of the house and I couldn't help but imagine I was approaching a medieval keep instead of a private residence. Four chimneys, each spewing puffs of white smoke, were situated at the four corners of the house.

I blinked once, but the house remained. "You sure this is the right house?"

Jake nodded. "Absolutely."

"It looks a bit like something out of a Bela Legosi film."

"Wait till you see the inside."

Ten minutes later, after we'd parked and made our way up the wide entrance stairs and through the house, I knew what he meant. The interior was like a hodgepodge of every vampire movie I'd ever seen. The house was so dark and brooding that I kept expecting a vampire, werewolf, or Frankenstein's monster to jump out at me at any second. Dim light flickered from a series of wall sconces positioned along the paneled halls we had to traverse to get to the ballroom. Jake led the way, and the closer we came to the wide double doors at the end of the last corridor the more I could hear the music and raised voices from within. The sweet fragrance of frankincense drifted to me on the air.

I spied numerous couples, singles, and trios grouped around the doors, milling about and conversing. Most were dressed like Jake and Dev in turn of the century suits and gowns with masks covering half of their face. To my considerable pleasure, I also saw that I wasn't the only person wearing a collar. There were three others--two females and one male--who wore one as well ... and we hadn't even entered the ballroom yet. Those collared were dressed differently than those who were not. Microscopic black latex body suits or skimpy black leather thongs seemed to be the preferred costume for the submissives. Looking at the uniformity of the outfits I was suddenly very pleased with my little red dress. At least I stood out a bit. But there was something to be said about a well-muscled man in a leather thong. The man's butt was a veritable feast for the eyes. Round, muscled, and so friggin' enticing I had all I could do not to--

"Where do your eyes belong?"

I jerked my head to the left where Jake was walking at my side and frowning at me. "On you or Dev … Master." The last bit came out rather hoarse, but at least I'd managed it.

"Then why are you looking everywhere but?"

I didn't feel like using the cursed title again so I shrugged.

"If I catch you looking around again I'll pull your dress up to your waist and put you over my knee. Would you like that, Stella?"

"No, Master, I most certainly would not." I said this despite the warmth suffusing my body at the thought of just such an occurrence.

He gave me a roguish grin that had an intoxicating mix of excitement and fear running hot in my veins. With a squeeze of my butt he steered me through the crowd gathered around the door, past the guy in the thong, and to the lip of the ballroom. "You look so luscious tonight I may put you over my knee for the sheer enjoyment of it."

The doors were closed and two men, dressed in very formal black suits, were perched before them, checking for invitations.

Jake handed his lead to Dev so he could pull the invitation from his jacket and brandish it for the guards to look over.

The guard to our right perused the small golden card, then set a meaty fist onto the door and slid it open. "Enjoy your evening."

The door opened wide and the air rushed out of my lungs on a sigh. "Oh," I murmured, unable to think of a better word.

Jake set his hand over Dev's on the lead and both men started forward. My only choice was to stumble behind them and follow, so I forced one foot in front of the other and followed a step at their backs.

The floor shone brilliantly under the crystalline light of a dozen chandeliers. It had been polished to within an inch of its life. The black and white checks were so shiny I could see the reflection of my red heels in it. As we moved across the room I tried very hard to keep my eyes on the backs of my lovers, as required, but I couldn't stop looking around. I'd never seen anything like it. On my left an entire wall had been fashioned of thick, frosted glass. It looked out onto a garden terrace decorated with stone benches, an ornate fountain, and artfully shorn bushes.

Couples glided along the floor, along the sides of the room others stood and watched. All were dressed in the same manner as we were, but nobody wore red.

"Jake and Cinder. I was afraid you wouldn't make it."

The voice was male and coming from somewhere to my left. Without thinking, I turned to look.

"Charles," Jake was saying, but I didn't have a chance to listen further because right then a sharp swat on my backside had me reeling to my right.

Top hat drawn low on his head and mask in place, Dev looked thoroughly disreputable ... and sexy. He raised an eyebrow. "You forget the rules so quickly?"

Unsure of what he was talking about, I blinked. "What'd I do?" I said in a whisper, then it hit me. My eyes had strayed. "Oh, sorry ... my Lord."

"You're desperate to be punished."

"No, my Lord, I'm not. I'm forgetful." Shamelessly, I stared down at my feet, pouted, and blinked becomingly.

Dev frowned. Then he raised a hand in time to clasp the newcomer's outstretched palm. "Charles."

Jake turned to face me, a smug smile lifting the edge of his lips. "And this is out little kitten, Stella."

Because Charles was standing near to Jake, I was able to get a few good looks at him. He was a tall man, pole thin, with wispy brown hair. His blue eyes narrowed when he looked at me and a wolfish grin appeared on his thin, colorless lips. The man looked positively predatory. "Stella. I've heard a lot about you." He glanced at Jake. "May I?"

May he what? I wondered and I took a step closer to Dev.

Jake's eyes lit on my face. He tapped a finger on the edge of his jaw and let his eyes rove over the copious amount of cleavage spilling over my clinging dress. His look was one of absolute possession. Being on the receiving end of such a stare was an entirely new experience for me and one I reveled in.

Eyes still on me, Jake nodded at Charles.

Charles slithered closer and held out a hand. "Sweet little Stella, how very nice to meet you."

I pressed against Dev's side and stared at the hand. I didn't really want to touch him. We were at a fetish party after all and who knew where that hand had been, but I didn't see that I had much of a choice. To refuse would more than likely embarrass my lovers. So I grasped the hand and gave him a firm handshake.

Still holding my hand, Charles proclaimed, "She's everything you claimed, Jake."

Jake disentangled my hand and held it at his side. "Was there ever any doubt? I have impeccable taste."

Charles spun to his left and roared, "Tomas, Drusilla, Edwardo, you must come and meet Jake's newest acquisition. He and Cinder's little pet slave."

I bit my lip so hard I wouldn't have been surprised if I'd tasted blood. Newest acquisition? Little pet slave! Where the hell did this man get off calling me a pet slave? I was itching to knee the asshole in the balls.

Jake must have sensed this because he gave my hand a firm squeeze. "You all right?" he asked in a low voice.

I had to remind myself that I was there for Jake and Dev, not that idiot, and I would have a good time despite him. "That man's a dumb ass," I mumbled under my breath.

Smiling, Jake swiveled toward me and bent to my ear. "You're right. Would you like me to kick his ass for you?"

Though I knew he was joking, his eyes glimmered with hope. Even as he was speaking I couldn't miss the fact that he'd slipped his free hand into the inner pocket of his jacket where he'd placed the red paddle. "No, you don't have to kick his ass," I said into his ear.

When Jake stood to his full height, I saw that a small crowd had gathered around us. It seemed they had approached with the express purpose of having a look at Jake's "newest acquisition."

I allowed myself a few seconds to look at the collection of fetish revelers. Each had come in a black tux or dress and had a black mask affixed to his or her face. They were a multi-cultural array of masters and mistresses, none of them overly attractive. Not like Jake and Dev. It wasn't a wonder they were taking such an interest Jake, beauty that he was.

I dropped my gaze to my feet and nearly cried out. Four people were kneeling on the floor. From their collars and leads I gathered they were slaves, but for the life of me I couldn't figure out why they were on their knees. I was collared too, after all, and neither Jake nor Dev had made me crawl about on the floor. Did these slaves prefer to move about on all fours?

I chanced a look at Dev, eyebrow raised, but he wasn't looking at me. He was too busy listening to some guy in a tux gush over Jake's good fortune.

"It really isn't fair," the guy was saying. Curious, I chanced a look at him. "First you managed attaching yourself to one of Baltimore's sexiest men." Pale haired and clearly enamored of Dev, the guy practically drooled on Dev's boots as he spoke. "Now you and Cinder have acquired this delectable little morsel. And she's so well behaved. How do you do it?"

Jake glanced at me, then Dev. "I'm irresistible. Isn't that right, Cinder?"

Dev tipped his hat to Jake, bowing slightly at the waist. "You're absolutely magnificent, Jake."

"And she's very lovely, isn't she," a female said. Instead of looking up to see if Kathleen Turner had entered the room, I fixed my eyes to my shoes and focused on breathing. "May we see her face?"

A moment later, Jake nudged my chin with an index finger and forced me to lift my head. This was disturbing on many levels. For one, where was I supposed to look? Was it okay to look at the idiots gathered around me or was I supposed to keep my eyes on Jake or Dev. For another thing, I didn't like feeling like I was on display. Was I their lover or a sex trophy? I couldn't imagine if they saw me as their lover they would present me like this to their friends. It was humiliating.

Still, I tried my best to look becoming, just as I knew Jake and Dev wanted. It was proving difficult. Time seemed to ebb as my face was stared at and my body commented on. The effort of control was nearly impossible to maintain.

"What lovely lips," the woman was saying. "What lovely, kissable lips."

"And those breasts," a man said from my left. "Have you ever seen such perfect breasts? Not including yours, of course, darling. May we touch them, Jake?"

"No," Jake said, quickly.

"Possessive are we?" someone else asked.

"Very."

I was desperate to get away from these people and humiliated beyond words. Why the hell were Jake and Dev just standing there, going along with this? Why didn't they do something?

The woman oozed closer. "How old is she? She looks so innocent, so sweet. Is this your first time at a ball, honey?"

"You know better than that, Drusilla," Jake admonished. "If you're trying to trick her into speaking, it won't work."

The woman harrumphed. "I really would love to see her spanked. She has a wonderful body. Are you sure I can't touch her, Jake? Touch one of those lovely brown nipples?"

"How lovely," a new voice announced. "Is that a tear? Is she crying? How I love it when they cry."

Shit! I bit my lower lip to keep it from trembling and wobbling like a five-year- old would have, but it didn't help. I was crying and everyone knew it. So far only one tear had managed to escape, but one was enough. I wasn't the sexy lover Jake and Dev had hoped I'd be tonight and I was doing a great job at embarrassing them.

"Come kitten, dance with me." Dev, who was still holding my lead, slipped his hand around my waist and led me away from the gathering and toward the center of the ballroom where couples were moving over an oval dance floor, gliding in circles to Elliot Goldenthal's *Santiago's Waltz* which was being played vigorously by a small orchestra. Dev guided me onto the floor. "Are you all right?" he said as soon as we were moving along the floor.

I swallowed down a sob and struggled to hold tight to my composure. "I'm sorry. I know I embarrassed you."

"You haven't done anything to be sorry for, Stella. They should be sorry, not you. They were like a bunch of sharks. I've never seen them behave so horribly." His voice had a hard edge. His breathing was harsh, his eyes narrowed and his brows drawn low. I knew at once he hadn't enjoyed their scrutiny any more than me. "I would have pulled you away sooner but I didn't realize you were upset. I'm sorry, Stella."

"It's not your fault."

He cupped the back of my head in his hand and gently pressed my face into his chest. "My sweet little Stella," he said into the top of my head.

We moved across the floor, my face hidden in the lapels of his jacket and he with his arms tight around me. He held me close to him until the next song began and he saw Jake waiting for us at the edge of the dance floor. "Let's go. Jake's waiting."

Though I followed Dev, there was a part of me that wanted to remain where I was and refuse to move. I didn't want to know what Jake had thought of my performance. Dev may not have been offended, but Jake tended to be less understanding than Dev.

We reached Jake just as I recognized **Edvard Grieg**'s *In the Hall of the Mountain King.*

"Are you all right, Stella?" Jake brushed the edge of my eyelid with his thumb. He'd spoken so softly that I almost hadn't heard him over the music. He was staring at me, head tilted, concern etched in the creases of his forehead. "I'm sorry I put you through that. We shouldn't have brought you here so soon. I should have known they'd behave--"

"Like pigs," Dev supplied.

"Exactly."

"I'm sorry I embarrassed you," I said.

Jake snorted. "You didn't embarrass me. I don't care what they think. And anyway, they were so charmed by your tears they hardly knew what to do with themselves. They dragged their slaves off shortly after you left. Care to guess what they're doing with them right now."

"Did they make their subs crawl on all fours?"

"Some subs get off on that." He held his arm out for me. "Let's go home."

Though I was more than ready to leave, I felt bad about ruining the evening. They'd been looking forward to this ball for weeks. "But we just got here."

It was Dev's turn to snort. "Big deal. I'd rather be at home where I can have you both to myself."

Well, I couldn't argue with that.

* * * *

1:07 AM

I lay between my lovers, eyes fixed on the glowing flames in the fireplace. We hadn't made love when we'd gotten home. They seemed to sense I wasn't in the mood for sex after my experience at the ball. Instead, we changed into comfortable clothes, put on the CD player and listened to Kim Water, Paul Hardcastle, and Paul Taylor. As I sat in bed listening the mellow jazz of Kim Waters I began to wonder why I was making such a big deal about our triad. Jake and Dev cared about me and would never do anything to hurt me. I knew that more tonight than ever.

They wouldn't hurt me.

And I trusted them. I was, in fact, falling in love with them.

Mom had to meet them sometime. What better day than my birthday? And so, I decided to have anal sex with them.

Chapter Seventeen

Journal Entry 1/9/05, 2:01 PM

I sat comfortably between Jake and Dev, a bowl of unbuttered popcorn balanced on my thighs. Though I was holding the snack, the two massive hands constantly buried in its depths prevented me from having much. Couldn't say I minded, though. Thanks to Jake, the popcorn pretty much sucked. It was low sodium, no butter, and no taste! He caught me trying to dump a half-cup of melted butter into it and nearly had a meltdown.

We were sitting in the living room, watching Spider-Man 2, I was trying my damnedest to figure out an appropriate time to tell them I'd decided to give anal sex a try, but couldn't seem to find the right moment. Already we'd sat through some B-rate horror movie.

Anyway, we'd just watched that amazing train/fight scene in Spiderman and I was busy trying to figure out how best to broach the subject of anal sex, when Dev's voice broke into my thoughts.

"How's the wedding coming?" He asked.

On my right, Jake grumbled.

"Ann's?"

Dev nodded. "Did they set a date yet?"

"Gerard wants the summer but Ann says summer weddings are tired and overdone."

Jake poked me in the ribs and scowled. "Do you two mind? I'm trying to watch the movie. Can't you talk about this later?"

"I think Ann's right," Dev continued, winning more swears from Jake's corner of the sofa. "Getting married in June or July would be trite. If I were Ann, I'd do it in October."

"Ooh," I purred. "And her bridesmaids can wear orange. I look good in orange."

"A sexy orange and black gown with fitted--"

"I don't give a fuck if they wear orange, black, or candy apple red. I'm trying to watch a movie. Could you both be quiet?"

Dev looked defiant. I leaned in close and whispered, "Is he always like this during movies?"

Dev shook his head. "Worse. He hates when anyone talks when he's watching--"

"Dev!" Jake demanded.

Dev and I fell silent.

I returned to thoughts of anal sex. As I considered the best ways of raising the subject I studied Spiderman's suit, various alluring ideas running through my head. I wondered how Jake and Dev would look in the Spiderman suit. With their tight asses and sculpted bodies, they'd be a sight amazing enough to leave a girl crying. I could nearly see the tight spandex melding to their backsides.

Tobey Maguire looked all right in the Spidey suit, but he couldn't fill it out the way Jake and Dev could. What could I do to do to persuade them a little game of Spiderman would be fun?

My pleasant thoughts were rudely interrupted when Dev bolted upright and raised a brow at me. "Don't you think you're spending an inordinate amount of time looking at him?"

I frowned. "What?"

"You're staring at Spiderman's ass."

"Am not."

"You are. I've been watching you the whole time."

I rolled my eyes, something I did whenever I was preparing to lie. "I was not staring at Spiderman's ass. Spiderman's practically a kid."

"And you were staring at that kid's ass. Face it Stella, you're a sexual deviant. What is he, twenty-one, twenty-two?"

For a while, Jake managed to refrain from comment. Then he took in a deep breath and prepared to yell.

Deciding it was now or never, I swallowed. Finding the remote on the coffee table I clenched it in one hand, hit the off button, and then tossed it aside. The screen went black and the room fell silent. "I've come to a decision," I said quickly.

Jake set his glass on the table, and then waited. Dev twisted around on the sofa so he sat facing me. Eyes bright with interest, Dev leaned back on the heels of his hands.

Focusing my attention on the floor, I began. "I'll try the anal thing," I said, feeling incredibly stupid to hear the word anal come out my mouth. "I trust you both, and know you'll do your best to make it feel good for me, so I figured what the hell! Might as well give it a go. You know, I might actually like it. Cause, you know, if someone had told me in early January that I'd get off on domination sex I would have thought they'd lost their mind. But here I am." I shrugged. "Getting off on--" I looked up and glanced around. "What was I saying?"

Dev stared. "I have no fucking idea."

Ignoring Dev, Jake asked, "Are you certain? There's no rush." Before I could answer, he stroked my cheek and tucked a stray strand of hair behind my ear. "We can wait."

I was absolutely powerless against Jake's charm when he went all gentle and patient on me. It was at times like this, when Jake seemed more concerned with my emotional well being than his own, that I knew how much he truly cared about me.

Leaning into his hand and breathing in the musky scent that was uniquely Jake, I allowed myself a moment to revel in his touch. I let this bizarre sensation--that I was truly cared for--wash over me. A few seconds later, I opened my eyes and met Jake's intent emerald gaze. "I'm ready. Let's go upstairs."

* * * *

2:39 PM

I lay on my stomach, naked but for my ruby pinky ring and a sterling silver necklace. Despite the small inferno blazing in the fireplace and the heat coming through various vents around the room, I couldn't stop shivering. My toes were icy, my fingers stiff with a bitter chill, and I had gooseflesh all along my arms. I wasn't cold, at least not in the normal sense. But I was scared ... petrified of what was coming. How bad would it hurt to have an erect penis shoved up my butt?

Another chill danced up my spine and I shivered.

Beside me, Dev hoisted me onto his lap, so my face was resting comfortably against his naked thigh. As though he'd known how terrified I was of the mere prospect of anal sex, Dev had been chattering since we got in the room. Now, he slid his fingers through my hair and began to massage my scalp.

The gentle pressure of his fingers as he rhythmically moved them over my skin was like paradise. Moaning softly, I burrowed closer.

"I decided to use the name Cinder," Dev was saying, "because there already was a band whose singer called himself Blaze. In retrospect, Blaze sounds a bit like a feminine name. Don't you think?"

"Dev?" I interrupted.

For a moment, his hands stilled. But only for a moment. A few seconds ticked by, then he asked, "Yeah?"

"I know you both would like to--" I let the sentence trail off as I searched for the right words.

"You'd rather just have Jake tonight."

I would have nodded, but what he was doing to my scalp felt so good, I didn't want to move. "Yeah. I kinda just want to focus on the anal thing. I'm thinking I may be a little sore afterwards, and a little tired so it might be good if we hold off on doing anything else for a few hours. Is that all right with you?"

When he began to laugh I couldn't help but twist around so I could stare up at him.

"I'm sorry, Stella," he began, "but you make us sound like sexual predators instead of your lovers. If you're sore or tired we're not going to force sex on you. We're not like that. You should know that by now."

Feeling chastised, I subsided against his lap and frowned. "I'm sorry. You're right."

"Of course I'm right. Stop worrying."

"What a pretty picture."

At the sound of Jake's voice, I froze. I told myself to be calm and take a deep breath, but the air wheezed out of me when I tried.

"I don't know, Jake," Dev began. "She's really scared. Maybe we shouldn't do this."

Jake didn't answer, but I knew he was close. I could feel him focus on me, knew he was devouring my naked body with his eyes, anticipating the moment when we were joined.

"Pretty little Stella," Jake murmured. He was standing at the side of the bed, waiting.

Slowly, I sat up and turned until my eyes lit on Jake's very luscious, very naked body.

Had it only been days? Suddenly, face to face with the wonder that was Jake, it felt like ions since our last time.

Hair hanging loose down his back and over his chest, Jake looked like a Native-American warrior god. His olive skin was flawless under the firelight. It seemed to glisten with a luminescence that added to the godlike façade. The muscles lining his arms and legs were rigid as granite as he stood, waiting for me. Most impressive of all, his erect penis stood at firm attention, as if eagerly awaiting the coming hour.

The fear I'd been experiencing receded under the force of sudden arousal. My gut clenched as lust turned trepidation into eager expectation.

Suddenly I not only wanted this. I needed it.

"Have you changed your mind, Stella?" Jake wanted to know.

I finished my visual perusal of his body and shook my head. "No. I'm ready."

"Good." Saying this, he climbed onto the bed and positioned himself between my thighs. He had to nudge them open with his knee, because I was still too awed to move of my own accord.

"Do you want her on her stomach?" Dev was asking.

Grasping my shoulders and guiding me onto my back, so my head rested on Dev's thigh again, he said, "No. I want her just like this. On her back and staring at my face." He focused on me. "This way, Stella, I can feast on your mouth while I take you."

"Oh," I chirped. Maybe this anal thing wouldn't be so bad after all.

Jake was motioning at something behind me. I could feel Dev move in response, then reach over me to hand something to Jake.

Baby oil.

"You seem relaxed enough," Jake began again, eyes on mine, "but I'm not taking any chances." He came forward and straddled my stomach. Again, he was careful to keep most of his weight on his legs.

I watched expectantly as he uncapped the baby oil and squirted a handful onto my breasts.

I knew what was coming next, so I bit my lower lip and waited.

When his fingers closed around my nipples, I arched back. Bright sparks danced behind my closed lids as, slowly, Jake began to rub my sensitized flesh. He massaged the erect peaks of my nipples until they were hard as pebbles and I was moaning openly beneath him.

"Like that?" he asked. An unnecessary question if ever there was one.

"I think that would be a safe guess," Dev answered for me.

He'd resumed kneading my scalp with the tips of his fingers. The combination of Dev's hands on my scalp, while Jake manipulated my breasts was nearly too much for me to bear.

A taut chord had formed within me; a connection between my breasts and my sex. Every time Jake flicked my nipple with the tip of his finger, fire raced along the inner channel connecting the two. A simple stroke was enough to nearly push me over the edge.

I was lost in the sensations rolling over me, drowning in the erotic thrill of their combined touch. They hadn't done much to me, but already I was beginning to lose my self-control.

As I descended into this sensual haze, I lost track of time. All that existed was the thrill of their hands on me, and the sensations their touch produced. I rode the waves as my lovers led me further outside myself. Fear, trepidation were forgotten as I opened myself to the endless possibilities.

I felt Jake ease back, knew he'd moved off of me when the weight on my stomach disappeared.

When he pressed the tip of a finger to my clit, and rubbed, I moaned. My eyes flew wide and I met his gaze. "Do it now, Jake. I'm ready."

Though he was breathing heavily, his gaze remained level. "I was gonna masturbate you a bit, Stella, but I think you're too far gone for that."

Pleased he'd come to the same conclusion, I nodded.

A slight grin playing on his lips, he focused on Dev. "Lubricant," he said.

Behind me, Dev shifted. Then his hand appeared overhead. He dropped a bottle into Jake's waiting hand. "This is gonna be good."

Jake squirted a copious amount of the lubricant in his hand then bent forward. A moment later I felt his fingers between my legs. He smoothed lubricant over my anus, rubbing gently to ensure I remained relaxed. His touch was tender, the feel of his fingers on me more pleasant than I'd expected.

After squirting more lubricant into his hand, I felt a finger prod my anal canal. The cool, slick gel oozed over my sphincter and inside as Jake penetrated me and began sliding his finger back and forth.

"How's that feel?" he asked.

I considered. "A little uncomfortable, but I'm all right."

He spread more of the sticky oil onto his fingers and began gliding two of them past my tight muscles. As he moved, I forced myself to remain calm. Though the sensation of being penetrated anally was alien, I knew if I relaxed and trusted Jake I would enjoy myself. Just like Ann and Meagan had said.

"Here we go, baby," Jake said after withdrawing his hand. He paused to rub his fingers on a towel Dev had handed him and then he came down on top of me.

The press of his body on mine nearly undid me. Feeling at the very end of control, I wrapped my arms around him and held him close.

"We're gonna go nice and slow, Stella," he said. "If it starts to hurt, tell me."

Frantic to get on with it, I nodded wildly. "Just do it, Jake."

When I felt his cockhead nudging at my entrance, I sighed.

"Push against, me," Jake directed.

Above me, Dev had ceased stroking my scalp and had begun to stare openly. For a moment our eyes met. He smiled down at me, raised a brow, then all conscious thought fled.

Jake eased into me, telling me again to push.

I did. Instantly I felt my anus forced open as he penetrated. Pain seared my ass as my muscles were spread wide enough to accommodate his thick girth. A cold sweat dampened my forehead but I strove for calm. I remembered Ann and Meagan's admonition to relax and push, and fought to do just that.

With a groan Jake slid in an inch, then another. Inch by inch he possessed me, filling me so thoroughly I didn't know whether I wanted to laugh or cry.

"Fuck, you feel so good Stella." His eyes rolled back in his head but he continued forward until the curls of his pubic hair were tickling my skin. "Oh yeah. This is good," he panted. "You okay, Stella?"

"Yeah. But don't move. Give me a minute to adjust."

Above me, Jake's hair had fallen over his shoulders in wild disarray. A curtain of sweat-dampened sable hung around his face, tickling my cheeks. His lips had compressed into a thin line and his face was flushed red. Trickles of sweat dotted his forehead and throat. He was exhibiting a Herculean effort for control. Eyes closed and arms trembling, he nodded.

I wondered how much power he had to exert over himself to keep from throwing my feelings aside and bearing down on me. "You okay, Jake?"

Jake grunted.

Feeling my ass had adequately adjusted to Jake's possession of it, I exhaled heavily and said, "Okay, Jake. I'm ready."

His eyes flew wide. Rapacious hunger danced in his emerald orbs and his lip curled expectantly. He reared up on his hands, balancing himself over me, and slowly withdrew.

Ecstasy came at me with sudden force. I dragged my nails over Jake's back, tried to catch my breath as he sank in to the root and pulled back a second time.

Furious heat seared a path from my ravenous quim to my ass, making me cry out. My toes curled and I begged for more as Jake began to move in a pounding rhythm in and out of me.

"She likes being ass-fucked," Dev remarked.

"She loves it. Don't you, kitten?"

I was too lost in sensation to respond, too overcome to think.

"What did she do before we found her?" Dev wondered aloud.

"Good question," Jake said and slid a hand over my stomach and between my legs.

With merciless resolve, he found my clit and stroked.

I arched with a cry of feminine joy on my lips. My stomach shuddered as something inside me began to give way. The most exquisite tension had begun in my sex, making me writhe beneath him. Giving in to wild abandon, I wrapped my legs around Jake and met him thrust for thrust.

I gasped beneath the force of his possessions, groaned as the tension built and release drew near.

"That's it baby," Jake crooned. "Give in to me."

Our eyes met. I fought to hold on, struggled to hold back my climax. But my control was tenuous at best. "Jake, I can't hold on."

He gazed down at me for a moment, then up at Dev, eyebrow raised in silent question.

"I want to see you kiss her first," Dev decided.

Without another word, Jake captured my lips and kissed me hungrily. Our tongues met and tasted.

I fought to hold him to me as he drew back, tried to hook my arms around the back of his neck.

Staring into my eyes, a look of triumph on his face, Jake bore down on me, driving into me with such force I had to grab onto Dev's thighs for stability. He thrust hard and fast, sending wonderful sensations tumbling through me. I whimpered beneath this delicious assault, squirmed, helpless against the rising tide that was threatening to overwhelm me.

When I was at the very edge of control, poised at the precipice of release, Jake grinned down at me and said, "Cum for us, Stella."

Something in my belly churned to a stop as my control ceased. Orgasm tore through me, erupting with a force that had me crying out. I shuddered beneath Jake, raked his back with my nails. Spasm after spasm shook me even as Jake cried out from on top of me.

He thrust harder, faster, groaning with every possession. Even as the force of my orgasm released me and I descended back to earth, I could feel Jake's hot cum filling my ass.

With a satisfied sigh, Jake collapsed on top of me.

I looked up and met Dev's feral gaze. "So that's anal sex," I panted. "I think I like it."

* * * *

5:19 PM

There I was, five in the afternoon, flat on my back, sticky with sweat, and exhausted from the afternoon's activities. My hair was splayed across the over-stuffed pillows and so tangled, I was grateful for the shut blinds. It was inhumanly hot in the bedroom and I desperately wanted to walk to the fireplace and douse the slowly ebbing flames. More than that, though, I wanted to pee. But I couldn't. As a matter of fact, I couldn't do anything. I couldn't roll over, I couldn't sit up, I couldn't twist, I couldn't even breathe. I surely couldn't get up and go to the bathroom. All I could do was stare at the digital display of the alarm clock and wait for Jake and Dev to wake up.

To my right, Dev lay on his side facing me. I could hear his soft breathing in the gloom and feel his rhythmic exhalations against the top of my head. One very naked thigh lay heavily across my stomach, pinning me to the bed.

At my left was Jake. Also on his side and facing me, Jake's breathing reverberated through the room. While I couldn't call Jake's sleeping respiration snoring, it was as close as one could get to snoring without actually doing it. As to his body in relation to my own; sometime he had not only set one arm over my breasts, he'd also entwined his leg with my left calf.

Between the two of them I felt hopelessly immobilized. The feeling was unpleasant, though I admit that it wouldn't have been if I didn't have to pee so friggin' bad.

It amazed me really. I wondered how they had managed to sleep together before. I couldn't imagine they'd been able to twist themselves into such intricate knots when it was just the two of them in bed.

I tried counting to a hundred and then backward to one, hoping the monotony of the exercise would put me to sleep and thus out of my misery. It didn't work.

I gave a go at closing my eyes and trying to meditate. I pictured myself on a sandy beach next month, the sun shinning on me while waves crashed against the shore. The imagery was good, until the imaginary sound of the water reminded me that I had to go to the bathroom.

"What's wrong?"

I jolted at the sound of Jake's voice. "Huh?"

"What's wrong? You've been squirming for the last ten minutes."

Oh well. At least I tried not to wake them up. "I have to use the bathroom."

Sitting up, Jake removed his person from mine, then reached over me and gave Dev's leg a shove. Motioning dramatically toward the bathroom, he proclaimed, "You're free."

I sat up, crawled to the edge of the bed and stopped. "Jake?"

"Yeah?"

"Do you and Dev like birthday parties?"

He smirked. "Doesn't everyone?"

I faced him, and smiled down at his reclining form. Hands clasped beneath his head and legs spread wide so I could see his exhausted cock resting against his thigh, Jake looked more gorgeous than ever. "My birthday is on Friday and my mom is throwing a birthday dinner for me. ..."

"And you want Dev and me to come?"

"I'd like it if you did."

For a moment I thought he'd say no. But he smiled and nodded. "I was wondering if you'd ask."

"Dev told you?"

"He did."

I grinned back at him. "Good. I'd been worried what my mom would say when I brought two men over, but whatever she says, I'm sure I can handle it if you can."

"Don't worry, I can handle it. So can Dev."

Smiling, I stood and made my way to the bathroom.

* * * *

Journal Entry 4/15/05, 6:22 AM

Crap! I'm thirty-one. How the hell did that happen?

* * * *

10:39 AM

Still thirty-one.

* * * *

11:22 AM

Still thirty-one. Guess I should get dressed. Jake and Dev are coming over to take me to a special breakfast brunch for my birthday. After that we're going to Jake's to meet Ann and Gerard, Katarina and Jim, and Meagan and Peter for dinner at my mom's. I hope and pray it goes well.

Crap! I'm thirty-one.

Chapter Eighteen
5:34 PM

We stood outside Jake and Dev's, shivering in the cold. Jake's black truck was idling by the sidewalk a few feet in front of Ann's and both car owners were standing on the curb, glaring at each other.

Yep, the evening was off to a fantastic start.

"I don't see why I can't drive," Jake said again. He was wearing a very suave, black and white button up shirt with loose black slacks. As usual, he looked incredible. His sable mane was loose and combed neatly away from his face. Though his jacket fit well, I could see the bunch of his muscles when he lifted an arm to gesticulate wildly at the cars.

Ann, dressed in a simple, sleeveless white sheath, rolled her eyes. "Because everyone can't fit in your truck, everyone can fit in mine."

"Everyone can fit in mine ... if we squeeze."

"Your truck seats five, mine seats eight comfortably. If Stella sits on your lap we'll be fine in my truck."

Dev sidled away from Jake, went to Ann's car, and pulled the rear passenger door open. "She's got a point. We'll be more comfortable in here."

"I won't be comfortable."

"Jake hates riding, he prefers to drive," Dev, dressed in his usual leather, slid into Ann's car. His lips were pursed as he scanned the sidewalk. When he found me, he smiled and gave me a "come here" nod.

Everyone eyed Jake.

He didn't look happy.

"You've really got to work on your control issues, Jake." I said and then disappeared into the truck behind Dev.

It was Jake's turn to roll his eyes. Clearly annoyed, he brushed non-existent dirt off his coat sleeves and lurched toward his car. "Big fucking deal." He hopped into the driver's seat, gave the horn a beep, then stuck his head out the window. "Dev! Stella! Are you coming or what?"

Sitting beside me in Ann's truck, Dev sighed. "Horrible control issues."

"The worse," I agreed. "So what do you want to do?"

"Oh! You think we have a choice?" He patted my thigh and began to slide toward me. "Sometimes I wonder if he'd prefer it if he were our father."

"You and me both." A little embarrassed, I arched my chin into the air and stepped out of Ann's truck. Big deal, my boyfriend was a control freak. There were worse things in the world, right? Like, hell, he could have been controlling and ugly. Or, he could have been bad in bed. So what if he was a little bossy.

Ten minutes later, when we were driving south on I95, Jake was in much better spirits. He'd been babbling excitedly since we drove out of his parking lot. "Don't worry Stella, your mom will adore me. I'm great with parents. What about your father, will he be there?" He paused, leered out the window. "Get the fuck off the road, asshole!" He jerked the wheel to the right and sent the truck careening into the center lane. "It's called the passing lane for a reason," Jake shouted at the offending driver as he sailed by the small, economy car.

Though it was horribly illegal, I was perched in Dev's lap in the front seat of the truck, holding on for dear life. Jake was weaving in and out of traffic, cutting people off, and cursing people out left and right. I'd never seen him like this. He was an absolute menace behind the wheel.

"My parents are divorced. My dad lives in Oregon," I offered, hoping conversation might calm his driving.

"No shit." He hit his horn. "Don't you dare … don't you dare … son of a bitch!" He slammed both fists on the horn. The loud *honk* was beginning to get on my nerves. "Can you believe that asshole just cut me off? Oh great! And he's driving two fucking miles an hour." The truck lurched to the left. As Jake sailed past this new offender, he held his middle finger up. "And even if she doesn't like me, she'll like knowing that I could take care of you," he said, finishing his previous thought as though nothing odd had happened.

He gave Dev and me a sidelong glance and smiled. "That I can take care of both of you."

Dev shifted. "Thank you, but I can take care of myself."

"I know. I'm just saying."

Okay, Jake may have control issues and he may drive like a jerk-off, but he is incredibly sweet. He wanted to take care of me. That was exactly the kind of thing my mother was desperate to hear from any man I was connected to. The fact that I didn't need anyone to take care of me was irrelevant. But since nobody's gonna see this journal but me I can admit that there's this secret part of me, an outdated and overly female part, that loves the idea of having Jake take care of me. Of course I'd never let that happen, but there was something alluring about the thought. "All right, you've persuaded me. I'm going to quit my job, move in with you, and make my life about making you happy."

Jake threw his head back and laughed. "That's what I like to hear. You move in with us and we'll keep you barefoot and pregnant."

"Ha! Dream on."

We arrived at my mom's relatively unscathed. I was a little shaken over all the near misses we'd had, but too happy to be out of the car to complain. Somehow, before it was time to go, I had to convince Jake to let Dev drive home.

We gathered in the foyer of the house with Ann, Katarina, and Meagan collecting coats and shoving them in the coat closet. I could hear smooth jazz coming from the back of the house where the room my mother insisted on calling "the parlor" was located. The soft hum of conversation blended with the music.

As I stood, gazing down at the checkered floor of the house I'd grown up in, my stomach began to do little rolls and dips. I was really at my mother's house with Jake and Dev about to tell her the truth about my relationship with them.

Had I lost my mind?

The men milled about the foyer, unsure of what to do, and I was at a complete and utter a loss. Between my morning with Dev and Jake, the argument of Jake and Ann, then the reckless drive down I95, I hadn't had a chance to think about what was happening today. The significance of the night struck me so abruptly that I had a sudden urge to snatch my coat out the closet and run for the hills.

"You all right?" Meagan squeezed my elbow.

The warmth of her touch made me feel a little better. Still, there was nothing in me that wanted to go through with this night.

I forced my lips into something I figured resembled a smile, and nodded. "Either tonight's gonna be great or it's gonna be a disaster."

A *clip clop* of heels told me the inevitable was upon me. It was her, my mother.

Crap!

A moment after I heard her approach, she appeared in the foyer, raven bob bouncing as she advanced. Her silk trousers were light brown and a perfect match of the cream-colored blouse she was wearing. As usual, she was accessorized to within an inch of her life, and as usual, she was gorgeous.

I watched her cross the room and was shocked by the unexpected rush of pride I felt. My mother was sixty-four, divorced, and more beautiful and confident than ever. If I had half her confidence I'd breeze through the night without so much as breaking a sweat. Unfortunately for me, though, I didn't have an eighth of my mother's confidence.

I was doomed.

"Stella! Happy birthday, baby."

I exhaled slowly, sucked in a cleansing breath and stepped into her embrace.

As usual, she hugged me so tight that I wondered if she'd ever had a career in wrestling. Her move would have been the 'bear hug.' She smelled of Poison and of food. Probably the roast my sister Reese had fixed for dinner.

"Thanks, mom," I squeaked.

"Lovely dress," she whispered into my ear and released me.

I had Katarina to thank for that. The moment I'd seen the petal pink halter dress I'd known it was perfect. Though it molded to my curves from the thighs up, it had a very feminine flare at the knees. The dress was sexy, yet modest. Very mom-proof.

While Ann, Katarina, and Meagan greeted my mother and introduced their significant others, I was busy trying not to hyperventilate. Dev set his hand at the small of my back and made me jump.

"Relax, kitten. Everything will be all right."

"I know." My voice was shaky, but I welcomed his touch. It was a small reminder that I wasn't alone in this, that I had Dev and Jake with me. No matter what happened tonight, I'd have them.

"And this must be Devlin."

For a good three seconds my mind went absolutely blank. Where was I? Devlin? Devlin who? Then my good sense kicked back into place. A second after that, dread descended on me anew.

"Stella? Is this your friend, Devlin?"

I couldn't do it. I couldn't stand there and tell my mother I was dating two men. I simply could not do it. It would be a disaster.

"Stella Marie?"

"Yes, I'm Devlin. Devlin Chambers." A hand appeared to my left. Dev's hand I realized.

My mother considered the proffered member, then slowly reached out to take it. "It's nice to meet you. Stella tells me you're a musician." Her lip curled perceptively as she said the word musician, and my dread of the night increased double fold.

"I am. I studied classical piano at The Peabody Institute in Baltimore."

"You did?"

He did?

"I did."

"Stella didn't tell me. Does that mean you have a degree?"

"I've a Bachelor of Music. I was actually a double major. I studied piano and music history. My father told me if I was going to make a career of music I ought to be an expert in the field."

My mother's head tilted to one side, and then something bizarre happened. She smiled. "Stella didn't tell me that either." The sour expression she'd been wearing when she got her first look at him slid away, replaced with one of cautious pleasure. "Come inside, Devlin."

She drew him forward and was about to make her way, Dev in tow, out of the foyer when she caught sight of Jake. "I'm sorry. Who are you?"

I cringed. This wasn't good. This was so not good there weren't words to describe how not good it was.

Jake, of course, didn't show a hint of unease. Confident as ever, he stepped forward, emerald eyes flashing, and smiled broadly. "I'm Jake Santos."

My mother released Dev long enough to clasp Jake's hand. "You're a friend of Stella's?"

"I am."

"Well thank you for coming. Since Stella left home I don't get to meet many of her new friends. And goodness knows the old one's hardly come around." She twisted and looked pointedly at Katarina and Meagan. "And I know you were just here last weekend, Katarina Beth. Your mother said so. She told me you were here to--" she turned on her heel, clasped Dev by the elbow, and strolled deeper into the house, talking the entire time.

Everyone, save Jake and me, followed her.

Was that it? Was she really about to stroll to the parlor where, no doubt, drinks were being served, without finding out more about Jake?

I looked at Jake, as though he'd know what to make of her.

"Let's just enjoy dinner, Stella. You don't have to tell her tonight, you know."

I nodded.

* * * *

11:42 PM

Why did I go? Why did I assume that since it was my birthday everyone would be on their best behavior?

Best behavior? I couldn't have been more wrong if I tried.

The evening started out nice enough. My mother led us to the parlor where she'd set up a sort of mini bar on her antique, sterling silver cart.

The expensive bottles of vodka, rum, and gin shone under the soft glow of my mother's three Tiffany knock-off lamps. The carpet was plush beneath my heels as I made my way across the room to greet my family. The muted burgundies and greens brought out the images of forests and flowers carefully woven into the sofa where my sisters Alyssa and Robin were settled with their husbands Greg and Matthew. Reese was stationed on low-back armchair in front of the bookcase on the far wall. My sister Jackie and her husband Troy were playing host and hostess. They'd stationed themselves behind the drink cart and were fixing cocktails for everyone.

I knew instantly by the lack of toys and food scattered everywhere that my myriad of nieces and nephews had been exiled to the basement, with those in their late teens looking over the younger ones.

Everyone wished me a happy birthday. I shared an Italian Margarita with Dev, and Jake seemed to be getting on with everyone quite nicely--probably because they didn't know he was my bisexual lover. We chatted in the parlor for about an hour, then, once dinner was ready, the celebration was moved to the dining room.

Thirty minutes later I was sitting between Dev and Meagan at the dinner table with Jake opposite me. My mother held her rightful position at the head and everyone else was scattered wherever they'd been able to find an empty seat. Dev had been telling us what it was like to be onstage at Nissan Pavilion in front of thousands. He tried to play his involvement down, saying Maverick was only a small opening act given a mere thirty minutes of performance time, but that was thirty minutes more than any of us would ever have.

No one in my family had ever met any actual performers before and they were making the most of this opportunity.

The biggest shock of all was my mother. She was on her absolute best behavior tonight. Not once had she treated Dev with anything less than respect. I couldn't figure out if it was the fact that he'd gone to school or if she was seeing that he did make a decent income as a performer. Either way, I was pleased.

My sister Jackie, fork poised before her lips, paused to study Dev. "You know what I don't get? I don't get how those guys managed to sing and play the guitar at the same time. Seems like too much to think about."

"Not really." Dev leaned over his plate, popped a bit of rice into his mouth, and swallowed. "You've just got to learn slowly. First you learn the melody, learn how to sing it, then you learn the guitar part. Once you feel comfortable you put the two together ... half time, of course."

"And that's what you do?"

When he shook his head, his chocolate waves bounced around his shoulders. "That's what I did when I played guitar and sang lead. Now I focus on singing. I'm a much better front man that way and it's easier to get the crowd excited."

"You said earlier that you're on vacation," my mother said. "For how long?"

Dev opened his mouth, but didn't get a chance to reply. Loud footsteps sounded beyond the dining room.

Jackie pushed away from the table and got to her feet. "Who's that?"

My mother stood and made her way from the room, talking over her shoulder as she went. "It must be Sadie. She said she'd be late."

Crap! Why in the hell was Sadie the cow was coming to celebrate my birthday? Probably she hadn't caused me enough of a headache the last time she'd seen me.

A tall, broad figure appeared in the dining room and I forgot instantly about my cow of a cousin. "Shit," I muttered. "He came."

Dev raised an eyebrow. "Your ex?"

"My ex from high school," I reminded him.

"Yes, that's what you keep saying. I don't see then why you should care whether he comes or not."

"I don't care," I said, lying through my teeth.

Steven, dressed in a very suave black suit, smiled to the table at large. "Happy birthday Stella." He was holding a bottle of champagne with frilly pink ribbons tied about its neck. "I bought you a present."

I was about to stand and thank him when, of all people, Sadie the cow glided up beside him sporting a grin the anti-Christ would have been envious of. In her nearly see through black dress and matching fuck-me pumps, she looked as though she'd just stumbled off someone's street corner. I couldn't figure out why she bothered putting any clothes on at all if whatever she wore was going to be translucent.

And where in the hell was Stanley? Why on earth did he let his wife run around town looking like a high-class hooker? She was someone's mother for crying out loud.

Meagan poked me in the ribs with an elbow. "Son of a bitch," she hissed.

I think I may have said something or did something to indicate my surprise, but I don't remember. All I remember is a horrid tightening in my chest as I watched these two, my ex-boyfriend and my cousin, make their way to the table.

Beside me, Dev didn't seem to know who to look at. Though I only caught a glimpse of him from my peripheral vision, it was enough for me to see his head bobbing back and forth between Steven and Sadie.

I would have been annoyed by the way Sadie was clinging to Steven, humiliated by the fact that though Steven wasn't interested in me he appeared more than interested in her, would have been mortified if Jake and Dev weren't there. But they were there and I figured if that was the kind of person Steven wanted, he could have her.

The annoying pair sauntered past me. "Look who I found outside," Sadie roared.

So they hadn't come together. That was something.

"Where is Stanley?" Jackie asked, re-entering the room carrying two chairs.

Troy hopped up as soon as he saw her, and took the chairs. "Where do you want them?"

Casually, as though she had no inkling of the disturbance she was causing, Sadie flittered around the table, dragging Steven along with her. She looked so horribly pleased with herself, so damned smug, that I wanted to slap her in the mouth.

"You didn't tell me they were seeing each other." Dev whispered into my ear.

"She's married."

"Oh, Devlin!" Sadie bellowed at the top of her lungs. You'd have thought Dev was a long lost friend by the way she beamed at him and threw him an air kiss. "You came! How nice for Stella."

Dev stood and shook Steven's hand, then smiled at Sadie. "I said I'd be here."

Sadie continued her circuit, giggling and smiling as she went. She was saying something inane about me and "dumb luck" when she came to a dead stop and began to sputter. "W ... who are you?"

Jake, accustomed to this reaction, stood to his full height and towered over my awe-struck cousin. "I'm a friend of Stella's. Jake Santos."

Sadie, the cow, stared at Jake for a beat, gazed at his hand, then began to giggle. She seemed to float forward, eyes fixed on Jake's perfect face. "Stella's friend?" Her hand slid out of Steven's. "Any friend of Stella's is a friend of mine. I'm Sadie," She made a point of leaning into Jake and resting one hand on his broad shoulder as she shook his hand, pumping it with tiny, limp movements.

She indicated Steven with a toss of her head. "That's Steven."

That cow! That stupid cow!

Rage boiled up in me, so hot and unfiltered that I wouldn't have been surprised to see steam rising from my head. If she thought she was going to sit there and hang all over Jake all night she had another thing coming.

How on earth was this happening to me? How? And why? What had I done to deserve this? Now I had to tell my mother about Jake, if only to get that hussy of a cousin of mine off of him.

Across the table on the other side of Jake, Jim nudged Katarina. I suspected he was trying to get her to stop staring at Sadie and Jake. It must have worked because a second later Katarina stared at me over her wine glass, raised her brows, and then refocused on her meal.

One look at Meagan and I knew she wouldn't be much help either. Even as I silently implored her to do something, she bit her lower lip and blinked. Hell, she was biting her lip so friggin' hard I thought she'd draw blood.

"Jake," I said, careful to sound more calm than I felt. "Why don't you come to the kitchen with me for a minute?"

"Is something wrong?" My mother asked.

"No, I just thought I could show Jake--" what? What could I show him? "--the woodwork on the cabinets." *Dumb, dumb, dumb!*

"Don't be silly, Stella. And you, Sadie, sit down and stop making a spectacle of yourself."

Dev slid closer to me and sought my hand under the table. "Jake isn't interested in her."

Ha! Everyone was interested in Sadie.

A low, animal sound rose from Sadie's vicinity. I saw the movement of her body, felt anger bubbling up inside of me as she eased closer to Jake. I heard her inhalation of breath and knew she was about to say something that would piss me off.

Lips set in a confident smirk, Sadie announced. "Please put the chair here, Troy. This is where I'd like to sit."

Jake managed to extract his hand, then settle on his chair just as Sadie was sliding her own chair close to him.

"Jake Santos," she practically moaned.

Jake blinked. His lips were set in a grim line and he began to drum his fingers on the table. "You were telling us about performing, Devlin."

Dev grinned. "Oh, I was finished."

"Devlin is a musician," my mother explained to our newcomers. "Perhaps later you'd play something for us on the piano. I've a baby grand in the living room."

"I'd love to. Do you have a favorite composer? I always say ..."

I fazed Dev and my mother out. I was too wrought up to concentrate on something as mundane as composers while my backstabbing cousin was making moves on my boyfriend.

Sadie regarded her plate briefly, and then sighed. "I'd like to know more about you, Jake. What do you do? And is Jake short for something?"

Jake continued to drum his fingers on the table. The more Sadie stared, the more Jake drummed. "I'm a fitness instructor. And Jake is my given name."

"A very masculine given name."

Good for Jake for having enough sense to know telling her he owned the gym wouldn't be a good idea. Knowing Sadie she probably would have sat in his lap.

"Where's Stanley, your husband?" I asked.

Sadie ignored me. "A fitness instructor. That must be why you've got all those muscles. You know, I've been meaning to start working out again."

"Oh, shut up, Sadie."

Dev squeezed my hand and leaned in close. "Relax Stella. It's funny really. He's at dinner with your family so there's no escaping her. There's nothing he can do. I think he'll beat a hole right into the table if dinner goes on much longer."

"It's not funny."

"You've got nothing to worry about, kitten."

I didn't respond. I was too sick and tired of watching Sadie seduce every male she came into contact with. Why had she even bothered to get married if she still wanted to play the field? Hell, at this point I didn't even care. The biggest thing on my mind was that she was not going to be playing the field with Jake.

Conversation rose around me, but I was too annoyed to pay attention. My sisters were talking to each other, the husbands talking sports, and my friends were catching glimpses of me, no doubt trying to gauge my mood. When Steven began talking to me, I was so focused on what was happening with Jake and Sadie I didn't hear him.

"Yeah, I'm Devlin," Dev was saying. "We've been together since January."

"Oh. So it's serious."

Dev lifted my hand to his mouth and peppered it with kisses. "We're very serious."

Steven glanced at me, then at Jake, and then smirked. He said something after that but I missed it. Just then Sadie's hand had disappeared beneath the table.

Jake's eyes widened and he jerked back and away from the table.

All right. I'd had enough. "What exactly do you think you're doing, Sadie?" I demanded.

"Stella, hon, mind your own business."

"Jake is my business."

"You know," Katarina roared, "I always say how good Stella and Dev look together."

"Yeah!" Jim agreed.

Meagan nodded wildly. "True love if I ever saw it."

Sadie leaned over the table and glared at me. "You already have a man, Stella. Back off." Her other hand disappeared under the table … and in front of my mother!

That just did it. That just completely did it. I shoved back from the table and rocketed to my feet. "Get your damn, slutty-assed hands off of him. You're in my mother's house, Sadie, couldn't you try to behave like a lady for five friggin' minutes?"

Sadie reared back as though I'd struck her. Jake's mouth fell open, and small gasps of surprise sounded around the table. I didn't give a crap. I was beyond giving a crap. All month Sadie had been itching for a fight. She'd gone so far as to show up on my doorstep and imply to Dev that I was cheating on him with Steven. I was at the end of my rope.

Sadie slithered to her feet. "Bitch! Slutty-assed hands? Who you calling a slut?"

"Sit down this instant," my mother demanded. "Stella Marie Rice, you sit down."

"You, slut! I don't see any other sluts in this room, do you?"

Dev clutched me at the waist and tried to pull me into his lap, but I twisted free of him.

"Oh, hell no." Sadie began pulling off her rings, discarding her bracelets, and yanking at her chain. "I know you did not just call me a slut."

It was as she was balling her hands into fists that I remembered something very important about myself. I don't like to fight. In fact, I hate fighting. I've never been very good at it. Sadie, on the other hand, had been brawling since she was five.

Jake eyed me, then Sadie, then slowly got to his feet. "Everyone settle down."

"Oh, I'm gonna settle down," Sadie continued, slipping deeper into ghetto speak the angrier she became. "I'm gonna settle my fist down in that bitch's face."

"Sit down, Sadie!" My mother yelled. "They'll be no fighting in my house."

Dev stood and inched in front of me. "Jake's right. Everyone needs to settle down."

"She started it," Sadie said, rather childlike.

"That's right she started it." I realized then that Meagan was on her feet too, her eyes trained on Sadie. "Because you're acting like a slut."

And with those words, all hell broke loose.

Sadie reared back and leapt. But even as she flew forward, Ann, in what I took for an effort to save me from absolute humiliation, dove for her legs. Ann drove into Sadie's thighs, hitting Sadie with all her weight.

Sadie sailed in the air for a moment, and then went down hard on the dinner table.

Glasses, silverware, food, and dishes went flying. Everyone leapt to his or her feet, staring in surprise at the bedlam unfolding at my birthday dinner.

Gerard let free with a torrent of curses even as he attempted to hoist Ann to her feet. Sadie was still intent on violence. I looked up just as Sadie was struggling to her hands and knees and trying to move toward me again. Anger blazed in her brown eyes as she tried to pull free of Ann.

"Let go Ann!" Gerard demanded, just as Ann loosened her grip.

Unexpectedly freed from Ann's grasp, Sadie slid across the table, off the edge, and onto the floor at my feet. She landed with a *crash*. Reese, Alyssa, and Robin tried unsuccessfully to dodge various sauces and dips as they were launched in every direction. The sight would have been amusing if I wasn't in the process of leaping away from Sadie. Steven, quite the opposite, had come around the table and was trying to hoist her to her feet. He had his arms around her waist, his body pressed to hers, and was grunting with the effort of trying to control her.

It was at that exact moment that Stanley, Sadie's estranged spouse, chose to make his appearance.

Dressed in stylish slacks, a white button-up shirt, and a leather jacket, Stanley sauntered into the dining room as though he were Wayne Newton walking onstage at the Stardust. The first thing I noticed, even running for cover as I was, was that Stanley had come without the children, unless he'd already sent them to the basement. Then I saw that he'd taken great pains with his appearance. His hair was perfect, his beard neatly trimmed, and he was holding a bouquet of roses and smiling.

His good humor didn't last, though. As I would learn later, the first thing he saw when he entered the room wasn't the pandemonium reigning within, but Steven "dry humping" his wife at the dinner table.

That's when Stanley lost it. Years of maltreatment at the hands of his wife came erupting out of him. He let loose with a roar of the likes I'd never before heard. He sounded like a wounded water buffalo. Come to think of it, he looked like a very large, very rabid beast. Even now, as I write these words, I'm not sure if it was the way the firelight danced across his face, or something else, but as he threw himself toward the end of the table where Sadie and Steven were, his eyes blazed blood red.

Seeing the peril he'd inadvertently put himself in, Steven tried to scurry away, got tangled in Sadie's legs, and fell flat on his butt.

Stanley launched himself at Steven and the two rolled across the floor, punching each other senseless, even as Sadie tried to wrap her hands around Meagan's ankle and pull her down. Troy and Matthew struggled to pull Stanley off of Steven. Jim and Peter were yelling about something or other. I couldn't understand them. And everybody seemed to be cursing.

I'm not ashamed to say I was hiding under the table where Jake had pulled me once he'd been able to get up and out of the way. We crouched side by side, Jake's arm wrapped protectively around my shoulders as we watched the disaster unfold.

I cried out in surprise when a high, sharp howling sound rose over the bedlam. Slowly, one by one, everyone came to a halt and looked around.

"You can stop with the whistle now, Alyssa," my mother said.

As if on cue, that horrid sound went silent.

Nobody spoke, nobody moved. It was my mother who finally broke the silence.

"Does anyone care to tell me what, exactly, is going on here?"

Nobody answered.

"Stella Marie Rice, where are you?"

Gulp.

Nobody answered, not even me.

"Stella Marie--"

"I'm here, mommy." I took a deep breath, then crawled out from beneath the table. When Jake stood beside me, I knew the time was at hand.

I searched the room for Dev, then spotted him. Steven had one arm slung over Dev's shoulder and was leaning heavily on him. Apparently Steven had hurt his leg.

"Stella?" my mother said again.

I smiled broadly. "You know I love you, mom, right?"

She stared at me, completely unmoved by my declaration.

"And I know how much you love me."

"Get on with it, Stella."

Gone was the happy woman of an hour ago who'd patted me on the shoulder and proclaimed that perhaps my choice in men wasn't so bad after all. Nevertheless, I upped the wattage on my smile and forced myself to continue. "You met Dev, my boyfriend."

Mama Rice exhaled.

"But I didn't properly introduce you to my other boyfriend, Jake." If I could have managed a bigger smile, I would have, but as it was my cheeks were beginning to ache.

My mother stared at me. Then stared at me some more. After a good twenty seconds of staring, she attempted to speak. "Your other boyfriend?" Her voice was shaking so horribly I wondered how much time I had until she blew.

Self-preservation the uppermost thing on my brain at that moment, I eased back a step. "My other boyfriend, Jake. We're what's called a triad."

"What a minute," Alyssa said, clearly confused. "You, Devlin, and this guy," she indicated Jake with one finger, "are dating? Each other?"

"That pretty much sums up the situation, yes."

Mama Rice turned slowly and walked to the edge of the room, speaking too calmly as she went. "I want you to go now, Stella. Get your coat, and your friends, and go."

"But mommy, you can't disown me, can you? You don't want to do that to me, do you?" I floundered then fell back on old reliable. "I love you!"

"Go Stella or I will not be responsible for what I do to you."

"But mommy."

"I will call you tomorrow, or the next day, or whenever I'm capable of talking to you without wanting to wring your neck."

I was going to argue, but I looked at Jackie, who was shaking her head. "Just go," she mouthed. "I'll call you later."

What else could I do? I left.

It was all one big disaster.

Chapter Nineteen

Journal Entry 4/16/05, 1:21 AM

I lay in bed between Jake and Dev, happier to be tucked safely between them than I'd ever been. A fire blazed in the fireplace opposite us and Jake had lit a few candles before we'd all stripped naked and settled in for the night.

"She'll get accustomed to the idea," Jake said. "There's time."

I was more than a little embarrassed by my behavior tonight and wasn't sure what to say. I'd started a fight with my cousin and unceremoniously announced to my mother and my entire family that I was in a triad. "Sorry," I blurted. "I didn't mean to go all green on you like that, but my cousin Sadie drives me crazy. And I didn't mean to bungle the situation with my mom so horribly."

Dev traced a trail over my stomach with the tips of his fingers. "Just give her time. She may come around."

"And she may not."

"Your mother adores you, Stella. You're her baby. I think she'll accept us, eventually. Just give her some time to come to grips with the situation."

Dev was probably right. I'd give her a week to contact me. If she didn't call me in a week, I'd call her and we'd go from there. I was not about to let my relationship with my mother go to hell in a hand basket. Annoying, controlling, and bossy though she was, she's my mother and I love her.

There was something very odd in all of this, though. As bad as the night had been, as terrible as it turned out, I was glad my family knew about Jake and Dev. I cared about them too deeply to want to hide our relationship from anyone, most of all my family. We'd just have to ride out the storm and do our best to make sure things turned out right.

"A tip from your former kickboxing instructor, Stella, you shouldn't go picking fights with people if you don't know how to fight. I think it's time you rejoined the gym. You're absolutely helpless."

Not this again. "I'm thirty. I don't get into fights. At least not usually."

"Thirty-one, kitten."

"Thirty-one," I agreed.

Jake edged close and slid his thigh over mine. "So what now?"

"What now?" I said. "I suppose we blow out the candles and go to sleep."

"Sounds like a plan. There's just one thing. Dev and I have been meaning to tell you something."

Shit! Not another crisis. I couldn't take another crisis.

Together, they nuzzled my ear and whispered, "I love you, too."

I laughed.

And you wanna know something? I think I believed them.

The End

9 781586 088859